SEPTEMBER TEN

J.L. Fredrick

Published by
Joel Lovstad-Publishing
2406 Columbus LN.
Madison, WI 53704

Printed in the United States of America

ISBN: 0-9749058-6-0

Other Novels by J. L. Fredrick
Another Shade of Gray
Cursed by the Wind
Aftermath
Across the Dead Line
The Other End of the Tunnel

Non-Fiction
Rivers, Roads, & Rails

Order toll-free:
(877) 634-4414

Cover photo and design by Joel Lovstad-Publishing

For all the people of Westby, and Genoa, Wisconsin

SEPTEMBER TEN

July 22, 1990 – Brooklyn, New York:

They made their way down the mile-long stretch of Brooklyn. Mohamed Bahajiman, Shahid Ahlimeskar, Ziad Abujarrah, and Imad al-Karim felt almost at home on the streets crowded with the city's highest concentration of Arab Muslims in traditional robe and turban. Men gathered in small groups at outdoor cafes sipping minted tea and puffing from bubbling hookahs filled with fruit and herb-infused tobacco. The newcomers had not expected to witness a neighborhood on American soil where the Arabs openly displayed their political sentiments – anti-Israeli signs and banners hung on convenience store walls, and outside an Islamic bookstore next to a mosque, a poster declared, "Allah is great—may justice come to the infidels."

Farther down the street they passed by the old Damascus Bread and Pastry. Arab men sat eating and arguing politics, just as they had been doing for years. Egyptians, Syrians, Jordanians, and Lebanese sat shoulder to shoulder, discussing their Arab-Israeli war experiences, the arrests of bomb builders, and the recent murder of the radical Jewish activist Rabbi Meir Kahane.

But on this hot summer day, the four newcomers' destination was a meeting with Emir Mustafa Shalabi, the director of the Al-kifah Center on Atlantic Avenue. He would arrange for everything, including their passage to Chicago where they would receive their assignments.

The tiny, shabby, second-floor apartment on Atlantic Avenue above a perfume factory was barely big enough for a desk, a few chairs, a phone and a fax machine, but through this office was funneled tens of thousands of dollars generated for the purpose of supporting the fight against the Soviet forces in Afghanistan. It was also the first secret base of Osama bin Laden's al Qaeda network in America, and an obscure gathering place for Islamic terrorists. Here, the red-haired Shalabi, a young Egyptian immigrant with overwhelming enthusiasm toward the Afghan effort, provided the four men with their new American credentials, ten thousand dollars each, and plane tickets to Chicago.

The four had met several years earlier while attending Sheikh Abdel Rahman's anti-Western lectures at his Egyptian mosque, a recruiting center for volunteers to wage jihad – a Holy war – against the Soviets in Afghanistan. With rebellious political interests stirred, they were ideal candidates for the militant training camps in safe haven Sudan, where Osama bin Laden had established and operated several legitimate-looking businesses – engineering, construction, and transportation companies – that doubled as cover for training camps. These businesses enabled him to procure imported explosives, and to transport his soldiers in and out of the country. His operation was a sort of clearing house for Islamic terrorism that would train and supply any radical groups, organizing their homegrown schemes into a worldwide crusade.

The recruits learned guerrilla warfare tactics, how to fire Stinger missiles, and how to build truck bombs. They were taught to create false passports and identification, and how to disguise their Muslim backgrounds by wearing Western clothes, being clean-shaven, and always carrying a pack of American cigarettes. By the time the four set foot on American soil, they had received the training that masqueraded them as quite convincing Westerners.

Early in 1990 it had been easier to pass through the visa system to enter the United States. The Berlin Wall had fallen only months earlier, and U.S. troops had invaded Panama in a hunt for the dictator, Manuel Noriega. While all this dominated the news, the CIA and FBI had relaxed their attention on the Middle East. Mohamed Bahajiman, Shahid Ahlimeskar, Ziad Abujarrah, and Imad al-Karim saw their opportunity to apply for U.S. visas in Khartoum, Sudan without any red flags being noticed. Unfortunately, the CIA had not passed on the information to the agent in Khartoum or the Immigration Service that they were on the watch list of suspected international terrorists. They easily slipped under the radar, and now they were freely walking the streets of New York.

Their instructions were clear: from the time they left the meeting with Shalabi, they were to *never* speak in their native Arab tongue, use their real names, or dress in traditional clothing. They had been trained to operate American-made trucks and to speak the English language as well as any Westerner so they could easily enter the American workforce.

Two days later, they simply melted into the Windy City population.

Friday June 1, 2001 – Fort Collins, Colorado:

Ben Hudson slowly came awake to the ringing telephone beside his bed. He suspected the voice on the other end would be Judd Avery, his boss at the construction company. Ben didn't really want to go to work that day, and even in his grogginess he recalled telling Judd that he needed a few days off after just completing final exams at the University. Squinting at the clock, he picked up the phone, disgusted that Judd would be awaking him at 7 AM.

"Hello Judd."

"It's not Judd. This is Bryan."

Ben fell back onto the pillow. "Bry? Why are you waking me up at seven o'clock in the morning? I just finished my finals yesterday and I need some sleep."

"Sorry, Ben... and for your information, it's eight o'clock."

"It's eight o'clock in Wisconsin, but it's seven in Colorado, you bonehead!"

In reality, Ben liked his younger brother a lot, and calling him by derogatory names was just Ben's way of showing his affection. He and Bryan had talked on the phone frequently during the two years he had spent at the University of Colorado. Those phone calls, every two or three weeks, were his primary link to home.

"Well, this couldn't wait, Ben."

Ben detected a little distress in Bryan's words. "What's so important that you had to wake me up so early?"

"Dad's gone."

"What do you mean? He's gone..."

"He's… he's… disappeared."   Bryan's voice now sounded almost as if he was sobbing, and eighteen-year-old Bryan wasn't one to get emotional to that degree.

"Bry? Quit foolin' around. What's goin' on?"

There was a short pause while Bryan tried to gain his composure, and then his words shifted into hysterical gallop. "Dad has disappeared without a trace. No one has seen him in about two weeks, and we can't find him anywhere."

Ben had always known that his little brother was full of the Dickens now and then, somewhat immature, and not always the most responsible person on the planet. Bryan had never been nearly as close to their father as Ben had been, but now he seemed deeply concerned. Ben sat up in bed, jarred by the alarming news that certainly didn't seem like the makings of a joke. "Bry… calm down and tell me what has happened."

There was another long pause.

"Bryan? Are you still there?"

"Yeah, I'm here," Bryan spoke softly. "I'm just a little upset, and it's hard to talk."

"Well, take a deep breath and start from the beginning."

"Okay… I'll try. Last week I stopped by his office after the last day of school, but he wasn't there. I asked Peter about him and Peter said Dad hadn't been there for over a week."

"Did Peter know where he might have gone?"

"No.   He didn't have a clue… just that Dad hadn't been there… and he didn't have too much else to say at all… like he was trying to hide something from me."

"That son-of-a-…." Ben muttered under his breath. He had never liked Peter Barrington, the new partner that had come into Hudson Trucking about five years before. There was always that element of arrogance, and although Ben didn't have any choice but to accept his presence, he couldn't understand why his father – Stanley Hudson – had let him buy into the business. "Have you talked to the police?"

"Mom called the Sheriff's Department and they came and talked to us about it."

"So what did they say?"

"They said they'd look into it."

"And did they?"

"I guess so… but they haven't come up with anything yet."

"So, how's Mom taking it?"

Another pause. "Well, Ben, what do you think? They haven't been together for almost three years. I don't think she cares too much."

"Bry… just because Mom and Dad are divorced doesn't mean that she doesn't care."

"Well, maybe she does… but she sure don't show it much."

Ben gave a brief thought of the last year that his parents were still together. It hadn't been pleasant, and he still felt some resentment toward his mother for her unfaithfulness to Stanley, the man who had given her a comfortable life for so many years. But Stan had remained steadfast in providing for his two sons, always being there to fulfill their needs and to share their joys and their sorrows. He had taken time out of his busy schedule to attend every one of Ben's wrestling matches, and he had been in the Madison field house to see his oldest son win two, back-to-back state championships. He made sure that Ben went to the college of his choice, and Ben was certain that he would do the same for Bryan. But had that all changed now? Was Stanley Hudson really missing? Had he abandoned his family and his business? It didn't seem possible.

"Ben? Can you come home?" Bryan asked in a meek, scared-sounding voice.

"Yes, of course I'm coming home."

"Right away?"

"It'll take me a little while to get everything ready and packed up… but I'll be there as soon as I can. Have you checked on my house lately?"

"Sure. Troy and I go out there every weekend to check on it. So when will you get here?"

"I'll be ready to leave here this afternoon, so I'll get there sometime tomorrow night."

"Okay. I'll tell Troy. See ya tomorrow night."

Ben hung up the phone and flopped down on his bed, deep in thought, trying desperately to put everything into perspective: Bryan had seemed quite upset, and he certainly couldn't have invented such an alarming story. But perhaps another phone call to Peter Barrington – as much as Ben despised the idea – would shed some light on the situation. He sat up once again and dialed the number for Hudson Trucking. Peter answered.

"Hi, Peter," Ben said politely. "This is Ben. Could I talk to my dad?"

"Your dad isn't here."

"Do you know when he'll be back?"

"No. Haven't seen him for at least two or three weeks."

"Do you know where he went?"

"No, I don't." As if trying to get rid of Ben, he abruptly ended the conversation: "Got another line ringing... have to go."

And that was all Ben got from Peter Barrington. But it was enough for him to believe there was cause for making the twenty-four-hour drive to Wisconsin. He would call Judd Avery and explain the circumstances, and he knew Judd would understand why he would be taking some extra time off. The apartment rent was paid for the month, but he would let the landlord know he would be gone for a while. He could drop off a mail-forwarding card at the post office on his way out of town.

As he cruised over the Rocky Mountain foothills to Cheyenne, and then across the seemingly endless plains of Nebraska, Ben didn't pay much attention to the landscape; his thoughts kept returning to the most recent letters he had received from his dad that mentioned some disagreements between him and Peter, but no more detail than it involved some less-than-honest multi-million-dollar negotiation with a group of foreigners. Stan had adamantly voiced his opposition.

One letter in particular stuck in Ben's mind. It had arrived early in May, typewritten instead of longhand as they usually were, telling Ben that he should stay in Colorado that summer and keep working, as the stability of Hudson Trucking was in question. Even the salutation at the end was typed: Love, Dad.

Ben was quite certain that his dad knew trouble was brewing. But had he actually written the last letter? It didn't seem like his style.

Ben pressed a little harder on the gas pedal.

Saturday June 2

Although Ben really liked Colorado and had considered locating there permanently, returning to his home state of Wisconsin was always uplifting to his spirits. This time, though, the circumstances offered little space for joy.

It was a little after 10 PM Saturday when he pulled his four-wheel-drive Ford F-150 into the driveway at his country house just outside Westby. Lights were on, so he suspected Bryan or his best friend, Troy – or both – were there to welcome him home. He had barely stopped the truck and opened the driver's door when a light illuminated the front porch. Bryan bolted through the doorway on a dead run.

"Ben!" Bryan called out softly as he threw his arms around his brother. Ben returned the hug. Words were not necessary for the two to understand each other's delight to be reunited. They hadn't been together since Christmas.

Eyes squeezed shut, savoring the embrace with his brother, Ben didn't notice the other member of the welcoming party approach. He felt another arm caress his shoulders, and as he released Bryan, Troy was right there for his turn to greet his best buddy.

"Boy am I glad to see you!" Troy said.

"It's great to be here and see both of you again," Ben replied. "I see my house is still in one piece."

"Well, of course it is," Bryan blurted out. "What did you expect?"

"That you'd probably wreck the place having wild graduation parties while I was gone, you lunkhead."

Practically tripping on each other's feet trying to be close after Ben's long absence, the three stumbled arm-in-arm into the house.

"Anything cold to drink in the fridge?" Ben asked.

"Yeah," Troy said. "I brought over a twelve-pack of *Coke*."

Bryan sprinted into the kitchen while Ben and Troy settled down on the living room sofa. Bryan quickly joined them with three ice-cold red cans.

"So, how are things?" Ben asked of Troy. "You done with finals?"

"Yep. Finished last week."

"Me too. How's your mom and dad?"

"Oh, they're fine. Workin' themselves to death, as usual. And they're anxious to see you again, so you better drop in and say hi."

Ben nodded. "And Mandy? You still dating Mandy?"

"Ben, we're *not* dating. We just go out together. You know there's nothing between us." Troy had always denied any serious relationship with Mandy – their only commitment was to be friends.

Ben knew that, but he would tease Troy with the issue now and then, if only to find out whether or not the situation had changed. His deep feelings were that he didn't want it to change. Even though Mandy seemed a nice girl, she and Troy would never make it as husband and wife. Ben knew Troy too well.

"And how's Grandpa Ernest doing?"

Troy chuckled. "He's okay... still forgetful as ever."

Ben's concern for the people closest to Troy was appreciated, but Troy sensed his best friend's stronger concern about his missing father. He, too, felt emotional pain, as Stan Hudson had always been like a second Dad to Troy. He put a gentle hand on Ben's shoulder. "I really feel bad about your dad."

With an empty stare, as if not knowing exactly what to say, Ben scanned the room, and then his eyes found Troy's. He pursed his lips tightly and nodded. "We'll find him...I'm sure." Then he turned to Bryan. "Is Mom at home?"

Bryan shook his head. "Nope. She went shopping in Dubuque with some friends, and then they were going to the casino in Marquette. Won't be back 'til tomorrow night." Then, as an afterthought, he added, "I'm gonna stay here tonight... okay?"

"You know where your room is," Ben replied. "How 'bout you, Troy? Will you stay, too?"

Troy pulled a toothbrush from his back pocket, holding it up beside his smiling cheek. "I was counting on it."

To hear the shocking news about his dad's disappearance in the wake of final exam week had left Ben exhausted. He had stopped halfway across Nebraska only for a two-hour nap, and the lack of sleep was catching up to him. The only thing keeping him awake for the past ten hours had been plenty of coffee and a generous portion of anxiety. But now, at home and in the comforting company of his life-long best friend, Ben could finally get a little rest.

Sunday June 3

Always active, energetic, and accustomed to a full daily schedule that usually began quite early, Ben couldn't sleep past 6 AM. He slipped on a pair of gym shorts and left Troy sound asleep. An early morning routine had started back in his high school days when he would roll out of bed for an hour-long workout before breakfast and classes. This daily regimen was one of the reasons he clinched the State Wrestling title two consecutive years, and although the intense training was no longer necessary, he still rose early. About three times a week he lifted weights, and the other days were for pushups, sit-ups, and deep knee bends. He enjoyed keeping himself in good physical condition.

But on this morning, he couldn't get past fifty pushups – his heart just wasn't in it. He sat in a lawn chair on the back deck, relaxing in the cool dawn. It was his favorite time of day, when the birds started chirping and an occasional rabbit hopped lazily across the back yard. Light, patchy fog hung over the hills, and the first rays of sunlight spiked out from behind the pink clouds in the east.

Ben wondered where his father might be, and why he had disappeared. Stan had always been one to face his obstacles and handled adversity with steadfast diligence. Running away from trouble just wasn't his style. There had to be a good reason for him to vanish, and Ben feared that reason involved foul play.

Bryan sauntered out onto the deck from the kitchen and sat down in a chair next to his brother.

"Mornin' Bry," Ben said quietly.

Bryan moaned and rubbed his eyes. "Did ya do your workout already?"

Ben nodded.

"What are ya gonna do today?"

"Think of all the questions I'll ask the Sheriff."

"When are you gonna see him?"

"Probably tomorrow after I talk to Mom. Wanna come along?"

Bryan shrugged his shoulders. "I don't know why you want to talk to her. All she cares about is the insurance she'll collect when they find out he's dead."

"He's *not dead*, Bryan. Quit talking like that."

"Well, that's what *she* thinks."

Ben detected a loss of confidence in his brother's attitude. Obviously, their mother had negatively influenced his thinking, too. "Well, I'm gonna talk to her anyway, and I want to see Peter, too."

"He won't tell you anything, either," Bryan uttered.

"We'll see. And what about Otis? Is he still around?"

"I haven't seen Otis since he quit driving for Dad."

Ben gazed off into the distance. Otis had been the company's best driver, and one of Stan Hudson's best friends. But just like all the others, he couldn't get along with Peter Barrington. So he had gone to another company. Now it appeared that Peter had, perhaps, planned from the very beginning to run everyone off, including Stan Hudson, gain complete control and accomplish an easy takeover.

But more important was the fact that Stanley Hudson had vanished, and no one seemed to know how, where, or why. Ben had been chasing all sorts of ideas around in his head all the time he was on the road from Colorado. Now it was time to formulate a plan to gather information and to pursue all the possibilities.

He kind of dreaded the visit with his mother. What would he

say to her? Although he didn't want to believe it, he suspected that Bryan was probably right: there were no longer any deep feelings between his parents, even though he had once thought they still cared about each other, but just couldn't get along under the same roof. He had seen them together having lunch several times after the divorce, and they didn't seem to be bitter enemies. But apparently, that had all changed. Since Ben had left for college, he rarely heard from his mother. He felt fortunate if she remembered to send him a birthday card.

Bryan was still receiving all her attention and care – until a month ago, he was still a minor living in her legal custody. That's what he had chosen when the choice was given to him. It was a logical choice; he'd never been really close to his dad like Ben had. Stanley and Ben had so much in common: hunting, fishing, and the outdoors; Ben had even taken an interest in trucks and the business, so there was much time spent together, whether it was at work or play. But Bryan was more the model airplane type, and although he tried to follow Ben's footsteps in sports, he could never quite measure up as his brother's legacy. That didn't make Stan love his youngest son any less – they just weren't close.

"Ya know what, Bry? Maybe I should talk to Mom alone." Ben noticed what he thought might be relief in Bryan's eyes. "And you don't have to go with me to talk to the sheriff, either, if you don't want to."

Monday June 4

With a little coaxing, Ben convinced Troy to accompany him on a visit with Peter Barrington at the company office. "You're more familiar with what's been going on lately. You might notice something that I would miss," he told Troy. Grudgingly Troy consented to join him.

As they approached the front door of the warehouse, Ben turned to his confidant with distress in his eyes. "The sign's been changed." He glanced back to the small sign above the door that read: *Hudson & Co.* "It used to be *Stan Hudson Trucking.* When was it changed?"

"Must've been just recently. I never noticed it before," Troy said. "Let's just go in."

To the left and down a short entrance hallway was the door to the office. They went in. Drapes were drawn on the windows and the light was dim. Behind the high counter a man sat at a desk against the wall, a large map of the United States above his head. Hearing their entrance he swung around and rose. An expensive-looking tailored suit hung on his short, stocky frame beneath a face that was neither unpleasant nor friendly. "What can I do for you?" he asked in an abrupt tone before he realized who was there. His glance darted past Troy and settled inquiringly upon the son of Stan Hudson.

"Mr. Barrington," Ben said and stepped forward.

Peter Barrington turned and stared, his dark eyes slowly widening. A meaningless smile spread across his face. "Why, Ben. When did you get back?"

"This weekend," Ben responded dryly.

Peter threw open a gate and ushered the boys into the back part of the office, pointing to a couple of chairs. They all sat down.

"Where is my father?" Ben demanded.

Peter leaned back in the swivel desk chair, drew a handkerchief from an inside breast pocket and mopped his forehead. "Why must you ask me that? I wish I knew."

"But Peter, what do you mean?" Ben leaned forward, his gaze intent upon Barrington's face.

Under Ben's piercing stare, Peter's eyes shifted. "It's difficult to explain. Everything was a mess – a dreadful mess! And your father is not here."

Ben moistened his dry lips, his face growing pale. "What... what has happened to him?"

Peter spread his chubby fingers in a gesture of resignation. "All I can tell you is that he came in here one day, said he was going down to the old shop to look for something, and I never saw him again." His fingers drummed nervously on the arm of the chair. "I know he went there, because that's where I found the company pickup truck." Then he turned his eyes on Ben, appraising the reaction. After a few moments pause, he added, "We've heard no word from him since that day."

Ben rose and walked over to the desk that had been his father's. He rested one hand on the polished wood. "I'm not a child anymore, Peter. I want to know how things stand."

Peter looked up at him. "Yes, of course." An uneasy smile flitted across his face. "Things have not been good since you went away." He looked at Troy. "Don't you think it would be better, Ben, if I talked to you alone?"

"No. Troy is my best friend. He's been a part of my life for as long as I can remember. He stays. Now tell me what's going on."

"Very well." The man's voice implied that he was uneasy with airing family secrets in the presence of a non-family member. "For some time business hadn't been... well... prosperous. You know, big companies taking away the freight business, and rising operating expenses, and then there were all those accidents with your father's trucks."

"Accidents?" Ben breathed heavily.

"Or so they were called. A couple of fires, one truck over the side of a mountain, one stolen in Texas... if you must know, it was the insurance money that kept your father's head above water."

"I don't believe that!" Ben's voice filled the office. Troy put a firm hand on his shoulder to calm him down.

A scowl wrinkled Peter's forehead. "Didn't you ask me to tell you *everything?*"

Ben sank back into his chair. "All right. Go on."

"The insurance companies were getting curious. And by then your father was on the brink of ruin. He came to me asking for help, and I simply reminded him of our original agreement."

"What agreement?"

"Ben, when I became a part owner of this organization, I had papers drawn up to protect myself. I had to see that my share was safe in case something happened. I had a lot invested, so naturally I couldn't afford to take chances."

The muscles of Ben's face twitched. "So, what are you saying, Peter?"

"I have nearly settled all of your father's debts in the business, and when that is completed, what remains is mine. There are no assets in it left for you, should he not return." Peter retrieved a file folder from a drawer, laid it on the desk and opened it. "Here. See for yourself. Your father's signature is at the bottom of the agreement, notarized."

Ben stared at the documents as he listened to Peter continue.

"If you'd like, I can offer you some money so you can travel back to Colorado. Stan told me you have a good job. Perhaps you'd be better off there."

Troy saw the anger building in his friend. "Yeah, Ben," he broke in, realizing that at all cost, they should avoid arousing Peter's interest in their suspicion. He flashed a glance into Ben's eyes with a message as clear as words: *Play your part, Ben Hudson. Play your part.*

And Ben Hudson rose to the occasion. With a little effort he smothered his emotion. "Okay. Maybe I'll take your advice, Peter; at least I'll think it over."

Ben staggered out of Peter's office – the office that had always been Stan's – and now it were as if Stan had never existed there. He had seen the papers that gave Peter Barrington complete control of Hudson Trucking. It seemed like a bad dream, a nightmare. This wasn't possible. Stan Hudson could not just walk away from the business he had nurtured from its infancy.

When they were back in Ben's truck, Ben turned to Troy and asked, "Do you believe him?"

Troy grunted in disgust. "He's too smooth. Wasn't he kind, though? Wanted to help you get back to Colorado."

"Troy? D'ya think he might've done something to Dad? I mean… maybe…"

"Now don't you go off imagining things." Troy recognized that he had to change Ben's line of thought. "How about something cold? Let's go get an ice cream sundae. I'll buy."

After the refreshments, Ben dropped Troy off at the house

again and drove across town to his old neighborhood. He stood at the gate to the front yard where his childhood recollections darted from every shadow. This was the house where he grew up. It was the only place he had ever called home until his dad gave him the old country house.

It had been ten months since he saw his mother; she was on a Florida vacation when he visited at Christmas. Although Ben thought there would be little information to gain by talking to her now, he also thought that it would be fitting and proper to at least discuss the situation. If she had just returned from the riverboat casino at Marquette, apparently she didn't need any consoling.

It seemed strange to knock on that door, but after he had removed all his belongings almost three years ago, he wasn't comfortable just walking in. It wasn't his home anymore.

Laura Hudson stood in the open doorway, taken aback at first to see her oldest son. She quickly regained a pleasant smile and stepped forward to give Ben a hug. "It's so nice to see you," she said as she backed away from the embrace. "I thought you were staying in Colorado this summer to work."

"I'm here because of Dad."

"Oh. Of course. You've heard, then."

"Yes, Bryan called me Friday morning. Why didn't someone call sooner?"

"Because we all thought he would just show up again... and we didn't want to get you upset."

"Mom! I'm upset now because no one called me."

Without making any effort to apologize for depriving Ben of the knowledge about his missing father, she said, "Well, you're here now. Come on in and have some coffee."

They went into the kitchen where Laura poured a cup of coffee and handed it to Ben. He took it from her, but remained standing, leaning against the kitchen counter instead of sitting at the table.

Glancing at him from her place at the table, Laura asked, "So how have you been? How's school?"

"I'm fine, Mom. School is hard, but I'm doin' okay. I should be getting my semester grades in the mail in about a week."

"You didn't come for your brother's graduation." Laura's words were cold enough to keep ice cream hard on a July day.

"I couldn't. It was during my final exams."

Laura looked away with an indifferent expression, as if she thought that hadn't been a good enough reason to miss Bryan's graduation.

Ben stared at her for a few moments. This wasn't the reception he had expected after a year's absence, and he knew, now, that there was no need to be delicate. "Bryan told me this morning that you think Dad is dead."

Laura's startled expression returned. "Where *is* Bryan? He didn't come home last night."

"Bryan is fine. He stayed at my house."

"That lazy bum was supposed to wash my car this morning."

"Bryan and Troy are helping me clean up the lawn."

"Troy! Is that tramp still sleeping over there, too?"

"Mom… why do you call him a tramp? He's my best friend. He's been my best friend since we were little kids."

"He doesn't even have a job."

"He would if Dad were still here."

There was a long, silent pause. It was easy to understand that Laura would avoid talking about her ex-husband at all cost. Finally she broke the silence. "I'm moving to Florida."

It was Ben's turn to be astonished. "What?"

"I've accepted a job at a real-estate agency in Tampa. I start there July sixteenth."

"But… don't you care about Dad?"

"Benjamin. Even if your father *does* come back, he's not coming back to me."

Ben just stood there, as still as George Washington on Mount Rushmore. That statement had said it all. She didn't care.

"And what about Bryan? Does he know about this?"

"I told him of the possibility."

"And is he going to Florida, too?"

"He hasn't said yes or no. He's eighteen. He's old enough to make his own decisions."

Ben set his coffee cup on the counter. "I've got things to do," he said softly, and started for the door. His mother just stared off into the distance. She said nothing.

All during the seven-mile drive to the Sheriff's Office in Viroqua, Ben kept thinking about the shocking news from his mother. He wasn't so concerned about her moving to Florida. He *was* concerned, though, about the decision that his brother would make. Bryan was not mature enough to be on his own, yet, Ben couldn't be sure that staying with his mother would be the healthiest environment, either. One fact remained true: Bryan was eighteen, and he should start learning to choose his own directions.

As Ben pulled into the Sheriff's Department parking lot, he realized how overwhelming all the difficulties in his life had become in just a short time. He knew he had to stay focused, and right now he would focus on his discussion with Sheriff Kent Lowery. He'd talk to Bryan later.

"Come on in," the sheriff said when he saw Ben standing in his office doorway. "How have you been?"

"Okay, I guess," Ben responded. "Considering the circumstances," he added as an afterthought.

"You must've just got back from Colorado, eh?"

"Yeah, Saturday night."

Sheriff Lowery offered a friendly handshake, directed Ben to sit in a chair beside the desk, and then he sat down, too. "I s'pose you want to know about your father?"

"Yeah... I was kinda curious why no one called me. I didn't know anything about this until Bryan called Friday morning."

"Well, Ben, y'know we didn't want to alarm you, or cause you any unnecessary worry. I figured Stan was going to show up somewhere... eventually."

"But he didn't..."

"No, not yet. But I still think he will."

Ben strained not to let his anger surface. "Well, I can't just sit around thinking that someday he'll come walking through the door. There must be something you can do."

The sheriff leaned back in his chair and folded his arms across his chest. "Ben, I've known your father for a long time. And I know how close the two of you are. Believe me, Ben... I had an investigator on this and we have checked every possible angle we can think of."

"Well, what about Peter Barrington? Have you checked that angle?"

"Peter? Why do you say that?"

"Because I don't trust him. I know that Dad and Peter were having disagreements over negotiations Peter was conducting with some foreign company. Dad didn't approve of whatever it was; he told me in his letters. And I think he had something to do with Dad disappearing."

"What else did Stan tell you about these negotiations?"

"He never gave me any details."

Silence smothered the room while Ben watched the sheriff scribble some notes and then asked, "How much do you really know about Peter?"

Lowery stared coldly at Ben. "I questioned him myself. I didn't find any reason to suspect him of anything. He seemed quite concerned about Stan."

"The only thing he was concerned about," Ben replied sharply, "Was to get rid of my dad from the business."

"Well, he never mentioned any disputes with your father."

"No. Of course he didn't," Ben said with a high degree of sarcasm.

"I'll have another talk with Peter Barrington," the sheriff finally said. "And I'll have my investigator look into it some more, too... okay? That's about all I can tell you right now."

Bowing his head, Ben let out a deep sigh. He knew Lowery was hinting that he should be on his way.

Troy and Bryan had raked and mowed the entire front lawn and they were sitting on the porch steps having a cold drink when Ben pulled his truck in front of the garage. He was glad to see they were still there. Surveying the yard and nodding his ap-proval he said, "Looks good. But you could have waited 'til I got home to help you."

"That's okay," Troy replied. "There's the whole back yard."

Bryan let out a little groan. "Can we do that tomorrow?" he whined. "I'm tired."

"Actually," Ben continued. "I want to talk to you guys." He stepped past Troy and Bryan on the porch and went into the house. They followed him into the kitchen and they all sat down at the table.

"What d'ya wanna talk about?" Bryan asked.

"I want you guys to fill me in on what's been going on lately at Hudson Trucking."

Troy squinted and frowned. "Well, ya know since Peter told me not to come in any more, I haven't really been paying much attention."

"Was that before or after Dad was gone?"

Troy rubbed his chin. "Must've been after, 'cause I didn't see Stan around there for a while, come to think of it."

"Why didn't you call me?"

"It looked like business was slow, so I didn't think too much about it. And I thought you knew. Didn't want to stick my nose into family business."

"Guess I can accept that as a valid reason," Ben replied. "But what about before? Did you notice anything unusual?"

Troy thought hard for a few moments. "I know that I didn't see your dad around the shop very much after Otis quit. I thought it seemed a little strange at the time."

"Did Otis and Dad have any arguments?"

"Not that I ever saw. In fact, the day Otis left I saw them talking in the parking lot. They were smiling and they shook hands when Otis got in his car."

"Did you hear anything they were talking about?"

"No. I was too far away. But I know they weren't fighting."

"At least they parted as friends."

"By that time," Troy went on, "Just about all the drivers were from Chicago. Three of 'em hung around the warehouse a lot – Lenny King, John Wolf, and Jimmy Belmont. And then there's a fourth guy, Sid Hollister who is the truck mechanic now. He came from Chicago, too. They all seemed to stick together quite a bit. I got to know them fairly well, 'cause I was washing at least one of their trucks every day. And Sid... well... he's there every day anyway. Except Fridays. None of them are ever around on Friday."

"Why not?" Ben asked.

"Don't know for sure. But they always take loads that deliver in Chicago early Friday morning, and Sid always goes with one of them."

"Maybe they just go home for the weekends."

"Nope. They're always back here by Friday night."

"Hmmm. That does seem a little odd," Ben replied. A logical reason for them all to go to Chicago every Friday – even the mechanic – didn't come to him. "Think maybe I'll look into that."

Monday June 18

Erik Wilson scanned the crowded eatery. The only empty seat was at a booth opposite a Luke Skywalker handsome young fellow sitting alone, looking more bored than lonely. He sipped at a large glass of soda, and by the number of torn, empty sugar packets piled on the table next to the half-full coffee cup, apparently he'd been there a while.

Erik stepped forward and then stopped. He took another long glance around the diner, hoping to spot an unoccupied table. There were none.

A curly haired waitress struggled to a nearby table balancing a tray the size of an aircraft carrier on her shoulder. It was loaded with more plates of food than there were people at the table. A ketchup bottle protruded from her apron pocket.

A strong desire to sit down anywhere commanded Erik's decision. Among all the strangers present, the young fellow sitting alone would surely not turn him away if asked politely to share his table. Erik stepped cautiously toward the empty seat.

"Mind if I join you?" Erik glanced around the room again. "The place is kinda full." He hoped the lone occupant would share the table.

As if double-checking Erik's statement, the boy quickly surveyed the packed restaurant, at first with a look of nervous astonishment spilling from his grayish-blue eyes, and then eased into a welcoming half smile. He appeared as if he'd just stepped out of the shower, his short fawn brown hair with that clean and wet look. A navy blue knit shirt proclaimed "Tommy Jeans" across the left breast in red and white capital letters. His broad shoulders settled against the backrest, relaxed. "Sure... I mean... no, I don't mind at all." He nodded toward the empty seat across from him. "Have a seat."

Erik nodded and smiled with relief, acknowledging the welcome, flung his backpack on the seat and sat down.

"I'm Erik." He extended an open right hand toward his host.

"Troy," the handsome fellow reciprocated, and accepted the handshake, but with little enthusiasm.

Noticing that a new customer had just arrived, the curly haired waitress spoke in Erik's direction while gathering up a few dirty dishes from the next table. "Can I get you something to drink, Hon?"

Hon? Erik thought. She doesn't even know me, and she's calling me *Hon.* "Sure... regular coffee, and could I get a glass of water, too?"

"Cream?"

Erik nodded his head slightly, remembering that he wasn't in New England anymore, and *regular coffee* here in the Midwest came *without cream.* His eyes wandered inconspicuously back to Troy whose head followed the movements of the other blonde pony tailed waitress, while a dominant voice at the center table told a trucker's tale about a narrow bridge. "... There was so much busted glass on the deck of that bridge – ya know, from mirrors gettin' knocked off – thought I'd have eighteen flat tires by the time I got across."

"There ya go, Hon," the waitress said as she set the coffee cup and water glass on the table. "Can I get you anything else?" Her smile melted Erik where he sat.

"No thank you... not right now... maybe later."

When he saw Troy's attention turned to him again, Erik tried to think of something intelligent to say. "Waitresses sure are friendly here." Not the most intelligent remark, but better than going into the theory of relativity.

"Yeah," Troy said. "But they hafta be... this is a truck stop, y' know?"

"Looks like you've been here a while," Erik said, scanning the table and all the empty sugar packs.

"Yeah, since about five-thirty."

Erik glanced at his wristwatch. Almost nine.

"I hang out here a lot," Troy volunteered.

"You must know a lot about trucks, then, eh?"

"No... not much."

"Then, why do you hang out here?"

"My girlfriend works here. That's her," Troy said. He nodded toward the blonde ponytail taking a tray of food to another table. The expression on her face was not a happy one, but she forced a smile toward the scruffy character, apparently getting up from his seat, and it wasn't difficult to determine the customer was upset about something. "Keep your damn spaghetti," he said loud enough to hear, turned his back to the waitress and stomped away.

Troy took notice of the mini-climax across the room. "Uh, oh. Mandy's gonna be in a bad mood now," he said with a silly grin.

Erik was convinced now that Troy was there simply to keep a watchful eye on his girlfriend. "You worried about her cheatin' on you?" Erik said, disguising a serious question with a boyish grin.

"Aw, not any more," Troy answered. "I did when she first started working here, but not any more."

Mandy paced back to the kitchen with purpose, carrying the steaming plate of spaghetti and a disgusted frown.

"So, then why do you hang out here?" Erik asked again.

"I sit here listening to all the truck driver stories... And if I'm here, Mandy knows I'm not out gettin' into any mischief."

Just then, Mandy stomped over to the table and put her

clenched fists on her hips. "Boy, am I pissed off!" her words guarded with a whisper to Troy. As if she flipped a personality switch, she turned to Erik, smiled and said, "Hi." But she wore that pleasant smile for only as long as it took to deliver the greeting, and then reverted to a disgusting scowl as she looked at Troy again. "That guy complained that he waited too long... walked out... and now the manager is on my case about it."

"What was it?" Troy asked.

"Spaghetti."

"My favorite! Bring it here. I'll eat it!"

"Is that all you can think about at a time like this? Don't you care that I'm in trouble with my boss?"

"Oh Mandy, chill out. That guy was a jerk and so is your boss. You shouldn't let yourself get so worked up over it. Now, can I have that spaghetti? I'm kinda hungry."

Mandy dropped her hands to her sides, turned quickly enough for the ponytail to slap her cheek, and stomped away again toward the kitchen door.

Troy gave a little chuckle. "Told you she'd be in a bad mood."

"How long will it last?" Erik chuckled, too.

"In five minutes she won't remember a thing."

Mandy came back to the table, slammed the spaghetti plate down and walked away without saying a word. Evidently, she hadn't forgotten too much yet.

The rest of the dining room tables were clearing. The dinnertime rush seemed to be easing and the noise level in the whole place had dropped to a murmur. Mandy busied herself with a broom at the far side of the restaurant while the curly haired girl refilled saltshakers at a nearby utility table. One of the last occupants at the big table got up to leave. He'd left the curly haired waitress a rather large tip, and he winked at her as he walked away. She blew him a kiss, and then turned to Erik. "Would you like something to eat now, Hon?"

Erik had been too occupied with the soap opera entertainment before, but now he realized his hunger. "Yeah, I'll have a cheeseburger and fries."

"Onions?"

"Sure," he replied, hoping that he'd had the last word.

"Pickles?"

Erik just shook his head in reply. He sipped his coffee and for a few moments watched Troy slurping in several strands of the spaghetti noodles. Sooner than he expected, the cheeseburger arrived. "Can I get you anything else, Hon?" the waitress said, retrieved a catsup bottle from her apron pocket and projected another warm-out-of-the-oven smile.

"Um... no... thank you," Erik stammered.

"How 'bout you, Babe?" she said to Troy.

Troy looked up at her, his mouth full and spaghetti sauce dribbling down his chin. He just shook his head.

For the moment, Erik had beached on an island of relief. This truck stop café experience allowed him to abandon the dark, dismal past; it let him forget about the insecurity strangling his very existence. He was seeing other people more clearly now.

He paced himself with the cheeseburger so that it would be gone about the same time Troy finished the last of the spaghetti; Erik always thought finishing a meal long before the other person at the table seemed a bit awkward. Mandy walked past and noticed the empty plates, stopped, collected the dishes, and carried them off. She seemed a little less irritable now, but not yet very talkative.

Troy's eyes wandered about the room, occasionally pausing here and there as if to make a mental note, and then continued drifting. His eyes narrowed to slits as the scan stopped abruptly at the front entrance. Erik, too, focused on the entry where a lone young man came in. Everyone here was a stranger to Erik, so it didn't seem unusual that he cast questioning eyes toward Troy.

Lingering just inside the doorway, the fellow glanced at his wristwatch and slowly slid his hands into blue jean pockets. Hair mussed and a shirt that had definitely not just come off the hanger, his eyes drooped from the lack of sleep, or maybe because of tremendous stress – Erik wasn't sure which. His gaze lacked purpose – like that of a politician who had just lost an election.

"That's Ben," Troy said softly, noticing Erik's puzzled stare.

"Friend or foe?" Erik was unsure of his own interpretation of Troy's sudden behavior change.

"Friend," Troy replied, continuing his gaze toward the door, waiting for Ben's aimless search to find him. Troy raised a hand, careful not to draw attention from anyone other than Ben. Erik still found difficulty in determining whether or not Troy was glad to see this friend.

"Ben's dad disappeared a while ago," Troy volunteered. "He's kinda been leanin' on me since then."

Ben's empty expression hadn't changed much, even after spotting Troy. He acknowledged the signal with a nod and slowly started across the room.

"Some people think," Troy offered, "that Stanley was in some kind of financial troubles and just took off to avoid them – and you know how the rumor mill runs in a small town? Somebody says something in the coffee shop in the morning, and by that afternoon the whole damn town knows about it."

"Well, was he?" Erik quizzed. "In financial trouble?"

"Not according to Ben. But he could be just protecting his dad's honor, but I don't think so."

Erik's frown intensified. Even though he didn't know Ben, nor did he know any of the details of the situation, he couldn't help but feel a little pity, although there was a little apprehension mixed in, too, not knowing exactly what kind of characters he was associating with.

Troy suspended any further comment when Ben was within earshot and finally slid into the booth next to him. Erik smiled and nodded a "hello" but thought he would remain silent until a formal introduction had been made.

"Hey, Ben," Troy greeted. "Haven't seen you 'round all weekend."

Ben acknowledged Erik with a return nod, briefly stared toward Troy and then waved at the curly-haired waitress for her attention.

"How ya doin'?" Troy asked.

With elbows on the table, Ben settled into the seat and rubbed his eyes. "Tired," came out amidst a half yawn. "Just got back from Chicago."

"What can I get you, Hon?"

"Just some coffee."

Erik took in the stocky, muscular form, arms and shoulders that gave evidence of unusual strength. He, too, was strikingly handsome, and it was Ben's worried expression that held Erik's attention.

The waitress arrived with the coffee and a smile. "If you fellows need anything, just give me a yell, okay?"

The three at the table just nodded and returned the smile with interest. As she strolled away, Ben reached with a handshake offer toward Erik. "As long as Troy isn't gonna introduce us, I'm Ben Hudson."

"I'm Erik Wilson."

"And I'm sorry," Troy offered. He watched the two shake hands.

"It's okay," Erik said. "Troy isn't exactly my life-long friend, so it's not his fault. I kinda barged in on him 'cause he had the only empty seat in the house. I'm sort of new in town, so I don't know anybody, and I'm pleased to meet you. Haven't really talked to anyone 'cept that truck driver who gave me a lift..." Erik realized he was rambling, and that he might make a better impression with fewer words.

Ben didn't seem offended by the overly generous verbal offering. "So, where you from?"

"I'm a Maineac."

"Huh?" Both Troy and Ben gave looks of subdued astonishment at the seemingly odd reply.

Erik then realized they probably misunderstood, and explained, "A little town in Maine... Pittsfield."

"Maine? So what brings you here?"

Erik gave brief thought to inventing a reason for his travels that sounded more honorable than the fact that he was simply running away from a life in his hometown that, as far as he was concerned, offered him little satisfaction. But then he decided that he could be truthful without revealing all the facts. "I was feeling all mops n' brooms... just had to get away from Pittsfield for a while."

The other two stared at Erik again, with curiosity dripping from their eyes. "Mops and brooms?"

Erik felt a little frustration, not realizing that he was using more slang unique to the people of Maine. "You know... out of sorts... uneasy."

"Okay. But why here?"

"This is where my ride ended. A truck driver dropped me off, and here I am."

Ben seemed a little less apprehensive with Erik than he usually was with people he didn't know. His apprehension had started when he learned the shocking news that his father was missing. But lately, his tension was affecting those around him. Troy felt it most. They had been best friends since childhood, and he was the first one Ben had turned to for moral support. Now it had become nearly dependency at times. Troy didn't mind being that needed friend, but it was beginning to wear him down.

Now that Ben appeared more relaxed, and was actually engaged in comfortable conversation, Troy asked, "So, what did you do in Chicago?"

Ben began to tell about his weekend adventure that had started before dawn on Friday. "I saw Sid climb into the truck with King, and I followed them to a warehouse on the west side of Chicago."

"What about the others? Belmont and Wolf?" Troy asked.

"They had probably left earlier... their trucks were already gone. But they all met up with King when he got there. They picked him up in a car."

"Did you follow 'em again?"

Ben nodded and sipped his coffee. "They went to a suburb called Bridgeview, a little ways southwest of the Loop."

Troy recalled telling Ben about the mysterious Friday absences. "So, did you find out what they do in Chicago every Friday?"

Ben nodded and sipped again. "They went into an Islamic mosque. Stayed there for over two hours."

Erik looked on and listened, but he had no idea what they

were talking about. At this point, it didn't seem important that he knew; these were just two strangers that he'd probably never see again after that night.

"So they're Muslims," Troy said. "But Friday?"

"Friday is the Muslim day of prayer. I asked around about that place, too, and it seems to have a rather dark reputation."

"Like, how?" Troy asked.

"I didn't see it, but I was told that the inside is filled with anti-American posters, and anti-American groups hold meetings and conventions there."

"I wonder if Peter knows where they go every Friday."

Ben just shrugged his shoulders.

Erik hadn't slept much in the last three days, and he felt as though he had traveled a million miles. He started yawning, and Ben noticed his eyes looking heavy. "Looks like you're camping," Ben said, nodding toward Erik's backpack.

"Yeah, I guess so, and I should probably find a spot to bed down for the night."

"There's a little park a ways outside of town. Nobody will bother you, and I can give you a ride out there if you want."

"That would be great. Thanks."

"I'm gonna talk to Mandy," Troy said to Ben. "I'll see you tomorrow."

Erik perched on top of the picnic table situated off to the side of a small parking area. The highway was quiet at this time of night, but occasionally the steady hum of truck tires sang through the darkness, and as far off the highway as this park was, the sounds of cars were hardly noticeable. Erik wasn't sure, but it must have been at least a half an hour since Ben had dropped him off. In the still, cool darkness, he felt a certain kind of comfort that he didn't bother to try finding the reason for, but rather just enjoyed it.

Somewhere in the distance, the cry of what Erik thought might be a coyote pierced the night, and somewhere not so distant a dog howled in answer. An owl hooted and the dog barked some more.

Erik gazed off into the darkness filled with the shadows of the surrounding woods. This was the first night since he left Maine that he had chosen to brave nature's accommodations. The trees, he thought, seemed more inviting than the all-night truck stops where he had spent the last few nights between rides. At least here he had a little privacy, and a balmy night under a star speckled black sky began to render its soothing effects. It felt good.

This park was tucked away in a little wooded area that was no doubt in the heart of farm country. There was just enough moonlight for Erik to notice several large boulders clustered among the trees, away from the picnic area. A layer of last year's dry leaves under a layer of this year's crab grass covered the ground, and there, between two big rocks appeared to be as good a place as any to make his bed for the night. While he fumbled with his backpack removing the blanket, he didn't think about being more than a thousand miles from home – alone, and with no definite plans for survival beyond this very minute. Instead, his thoughts were of his neglect to remember to pack a flashlight. Tomorrow he would get one.

As exhausted as he felt, he was too keyed up to fall asleep. He realized that his subconscious thoughts were of his life back in Maine, and he began to wonder if it had been a good decision to leave… or maybe he should have headed in another direction – maybe Montreal or Nova Scotia. He'd always wanted to go to Nantucket, but then, what would he do when he got there? What would he do here in the Midwest? What would he do anywhere? He had been just an average student – Bs and Cs mostly – but he had made his real mark in high school as a pretty good wrestler, but now his days as a jock were over. Now he was susceptible to life's hard knocks.

Erik's restlessness brought him to his feet again. He wandered back to the picnic table and sat staring into the darkness. The trees were nothing more than shapeless blurs standing silently in the still night air, casting their long spooky shadows across the empty lawn, the road leading in, swallowed up into the depths of obscurity. Trees had always formed a barrier of comforting security, a buffer zone between him and the outside world, but on this night, the darkness seemed to magnify his thoughts, as if he were a small child waking from a nightmare, terrified of the demons that had brutally invaded his slumber. Tears welled up in his eyes as the first whispers of an evening breeze gently caressed his bare shoulders. His entire 160 pounds was numb with an emptiness that he couldn't tolerate.

Three long weeks had passed since their High School graduation. To Erik it seemed like a millennium.   It had only been two weeks since Danny's funeral, but now he could only remember the emotional dizziness when he had heard about the accident – the fiery car crash on graduation night that had taken the life of his best friend. From that moment on, everything had seemed so unreal, so untouchable. And now, the reality choked him. His best friend, gone forever.

Feelings of sorrow turned to pity, to disgust, to anger, that gnawed at him like the jaws of a bear on a freshly killed fish; he couldn't remember ever feeling this low. His life seemed as empty as the lonely park and as dismal and dark as the night descending upon him. Danny was gone forever and nothing could change that.   Nothing could bring him back.   Nothing.   "Good bye, Danny," Erik heard himself say, and he realized he was talking to no one. But somehow, he felt a little more at ease.

Erik combed outstretched fingers through his short-cropped cinnamon brown hair and clasped them together behind his head. Now he knew he was forced to set a course; to find a direction – any direction – that would help him put his life back together. He needed a purpose.

A few days ago, he had needed an escape, but he had nowhere to go; the open door at his older sister's house, where he had been living for the past six months after his mom died, was about to get slammed in his face. Becky's live-in boyfriend possessed the personality of a hand grenade; he didn't like Erik, and it was clearly understood that Erik wasn't welcome in that house.

He had gone to his wealthy father, who had never really fulfilled the role as a parent, and since his wife died from a malignant brain tumor, he had turned to the bottle. Now he had become one who hated the world and everything in it. Erik hadn't seen him for a while, and he hoped that maybe things would have changed.

Erik found him in his downtown apartment, stumbling drunk and with no compassion toward his offspring who needed him more now than he ever had. But his father had shut him out when Erik turned eighteen, and now Mr. Wilson only offered more rejection, telling Erik he didn't need a punk teen-ager messing up his life, as if his life wasn't already in shambles.

Perhaps it was a weak moment during Erik's persistence that prodded Mr. Wilson to give Erik the only thing he understood – money. In a final attempt to rid himself of the boy, once and for all, he fumbled with his wallet, slurred something about three tensh 'n a twenty, and stuffed the bills in Erik's shirt pocket. "There's fitty bucks... all I got... take it an' git outa my life." And that had ended the visit.

An hour later, sitting alone at a diner, Erik remembered the money in his shirt pocket, pulled it out, and discovered that the three tens were actually hundreds. Three days after that, with only a few personal belongings, an extra change of clothes, and a blanket rolled up in a backpack, he found himself at a lonely, greasy spoon little truck stop in rural Indiana. Hitchhiking had never been his first choice in travel arrangements, but it seemed the most logical and economical way for him to get somewhere – and he didn't even know where that somewhere would be.

He sat nursing a bad cup of coffee, staring out at a dismal, wet day, and he couldn't help but think about his hasty departure. Guilt took over for just a little while as he thought about what he had done. But then Erik recalled the rotten relationship he and his father had always had, and $320 didn't begin to make up for a lousy childhood. Erik hadn't ever been the kind of person to use people for his own benefit, but considering the circumstances, Mr. Wilson deserved to get taken. He was the only person that Erik truly disliked. The one good value that he could extract from all this, was that his father reminded him of who he would try *not to be.*

He had always handled depression and rejection by venturing off alone, detaching himself from all others. But this time, perhaps he had reacted excessively... hitchhiking halfway across the country was a little different than the thirty miles to Bangor, or even the seventy-five miles to Bar Harbor out on the coast.

The rain had stopped, and there didn't seem to be any logical reason to hang around the truck stop any longer. With a little luck, another ride would present itself, and maybe the next town would be what Erik was looking for, whatever that was.

He had hitched a ride with a truck driver heading north into Wisconsin. Erik thought Wisconsin was as good a place as any, and he'd heard some people talking about how much they had enjoyed their vacation there.

They had talked at length from that point, about Erik's hometown, and his recent troubles, and his reasons for leaving. Then, after they had passed through Chicago, Erik realized how tired he was. He leaned back in the seat and closed his eyes. When he opened his eyes again, the driver was telling him this was as far as he could go. It was just getting dark, and they were in a small town in Wisconsin – Westby, he had called it – and *Central Express*, the truck stop café was open till ten.

Erik gazed around the park at all the shadowy, undefined shapes. It was as if he had just watched a movie re-run, and now he was certain he could go to sleep. He ambled back to his bedroll between the rocks.

Tuesday June 19

The gravel crunched beneath his sneakers as he walked along the shoulder of the highway that was much busier now. Erik looked at his watch – 8:30. He couldn't believe that he had slept so soundly and so late.

He had walked an hour to get back to town – far enough to work up an appetite for a good breakfast. He wondered if he would see Troy or Ben again, or if their time spent the night before would remain the only expression of a passing-in-the-night friendship. It really didn't matter, he thought, if Ben or Troy showed up again, or if their acquaintance developed into anything more than coffee shop elbow rubbing. He'd lived his whole life, so far, without them, and he could certainly continue on without them.

A completely new set of faces populated the truck stop restaurant during the morning shift. The waitresses were much older than the night staff, and other than the obvious truck driver crowd that seemed to be congregated mostly in one area, the rest of the morning patrons appeared to be older and more subdued than the bustling crowd of the previous night. And it was a much less interesting group – perhaps because this was the working part of the day, and these were working people taking a break from their toils, but not from the seriousness of the day.

Erik sipped his coffee while he waited for his breakfast. By the looks of the crowded dining room, he thought he might have a long wait. But what did it matter? He didn't have a train to catch.

His thoughts wandered, almost to the point of daydreaming. A voice startled him back to reality: "Found your way back to town, I see."

Erik jerked his head toward the voice to see Ben standing at the edge of the table, looking as if he were expecting an invitation to sit down.

"Yeah," Erik said. "I was getting pretty hungry."

"I drove out to the park, but you were already gone. Mind if I join you?" Ben asked.

Erik just nodded in the direction of the empty seat across from him.

Ben took a deep breath, scanned the room, and then sat down. He seemed a bit more nervous, now, Erik thought, as if he were afraid to be seen. "So how was your night out in the park?"

"Slept like a bear in hibernation. It was actually quite nice out there… quiet."

"Yeah," Ben replied. "There isn't a lot of traffic on that road at night."

Just then the waitress set a plate of eggs and toast in front of Erik. "And what would you like, Ben?" she asked.

"Pancakes and sausage… and some coffee."

Not much was said while they ate, but Erik sensed that Ben was eager to talk, although he seemed reluctant to start a conversation. After a long silence, Ben finally spoke. "So what are your plans? You gonna stick around for a while?"

Erik wasn't sure if he wanted to admit that he had no plans whatever. But the tone of Ben's question almost sounded like an invitation to stay. "Well, I might hang out here for a couple of days… maybe look for a job."

That seemed to lift Ben's spirit. "Hey, that's great." He hesitated a bit, and then continued cautiously. "If you need a place to stay… there's room at my place."

Erik was taken by surprise with the offer, but it did sound better than sleeping between two rocks out in the woods.

"And besides," Ben added. "I could use your help…"

"With what?"

Ben quickly scanned the diner again and then leaned across the table to speak in a whisper: "Find my dad."

Erik's eyes widened, and then narrowed to just slits under a furrowed brow. "Just what happened to him?" he asked in a low voice. "And what makes you think I can help you?"

Ben put a finger to his lips as a signal to avoid drawing attention, and continued to whisper. "Because you're new in town, and nobody knows you."

"But what— "

"Shhhhhh. Meet me and Troy at the far end of the parking lot tonight about ten o'clock." Ben picked up both food bills from the table and hurried off to the cashier near the front entrance.

Erik watched as Ben handed money to the cashier, nodding toward Erik's table. The cashier seemed to acknowledge.

Erik glanced at his watch as Ben slid out the door. He had nearly twelve hours to kill. He'd start by purchasing a newspaper, and then luring the waitress with the coffee pot to his table.

The local weekly paper was dated the previous Thursday. He thought he'd start with that. The want ads might contain some available jobs, and maybe he'd find something about a missing person to help him understand Ben's situation. Scanning every headline of every article on every page of *The Times* rendered not a clue, and because he was a complete stranger to the town, news about the meetings of the city council and school board didn't hold much meaning. The police report showed nothing more than a couple of speeding tickets issued by the local officer, and a dog nuisance incident.

The classified section in the back listed several available jobs. Erik thought he was qualified for at least three or four of them, and it certainly couldn't hurt to check them out.

By five o'clock that afternoon, he had completed six applications, but because he was a stranger to everyone, most of the possible employers didn't show much interest in Erik. Only one – Bert Greer – at the used car lot on North Main had given him any hope at all. It was only part-time, washing cars and maybe a little light duty maintenance now and then, for seven bucks an hour. Not anything too great, but it was a start, and at least Bert told him to stop back in a couple of days. That was more than he had heard from any of the others.

There were probably other places to find supper, but Central Express had become a temporary port, and Erik thought perhaps Troy might show up again, too. But it must have been Mandy's night off; she wasn't there, and Troy didn't show, either.

Erik hadn't planned to stay in this town for any length of time; then again, he hadn't really planned anything. And now, his new friends – at least he wanted to think they were friends – seemed to need his help. That alone presented a different concept, as Erik had not felt needed by anyone in a long time. It could be just a false alarm. Maybe he was just imagining the feel of need simply because that's what he wanted to feel. On the other hand, maybe this was all real. He couldn't think of any logical reason why Ben and Troy would make up such a story merely for his entertainment. No, the situation seemed serious.

He had a decision to make: stay and get involved, or wish Ben some good fortune and move on. Even though this wasn't his problem, it would be difficult to just simply walk away after Ben and Troy had so warmly extended their friendship.

He sat at a table next to the window and gazed out at that small segment of town visible from there. Tall, century-old pines stood stark and black, silhouetted against a purple dusk. The white water tower looked as if it were painted on a canvas of ominous charcoal gray sky. In sharp contrast, the brightly lit red, white and blue Amoco sign just down the street pierced through the gloom, alone, unafraid, astonishingly out of place in a residential area. It reminded Erik of a TV commercial, but he couldn't bring to mid the product it had advertised – not that it really mattered.

He had some time, now, to think about his options, and whether or not any of them fit his plans. *What plans?* he thought. By the time he had arrived here, his plans were no more established than when he first set out. He had thought then that traveling might clear his mind and help him seek some sense of direction. He'd had the notion then that when his footsteps fell upon the right place, he would know it.

So, now he had met some new friends, and there was the possibility of employment. Maybe this was the right place.

At ten o'clock, Erik paid his tab and stepped out into the dark end of the parking lot. For a few moments while he stood alone in the darkness, he felt a strange sensation that he might have fallen for some false expectations, or maybe this was a set-up. Out there in a lonely, dark parking lot he would be an easy target.

A pair of headlights came racing toward him from the direction of the gas pumps. He thought of running into the shadows between two semi trailers parked off to the side, but then he recognized the pickup truck – the same one in which Ben had driven him to the wayside park the previous night. He stood still, waiting for the headlight beams to sweep across the lot and reveal his position.

The truck stopped beside him as a cloud of dust rolled up behind it. "Hop in," he heard Ben's voice creep through the open window. Erik gathered up his pack on the ground at his feet, tossed it into the truck bed and stepped toward the passenger door that had already swung open. The dome light revealed Troy in the cab beside Ben. He jumped into the seat, pulled the door shut and settled back with relief that he had not been left stranded in a lonely parking lot all night.

After a brief period of small talk encompassing Erik's activities that day, and the impending stormy weather, Ben turned the truck down a side street, and within a few blocks they were headed out of town. "We'll go out to my place," he said.

Less than a quarter-mile from the city limits, Ben pulled into the driveway of a small, two-story frame house tucked quaintly between rolling hills. It had apparently once been a farm dwelling. A hundred feet off to the left was the remains of the stone foundation of a barn, mostly hidden by weeds. To the right stood a two-car garage that Ben aimed the truck toward. In front of one of the garage doors was a multi-colored Ford Mustang.

"Well, Troy," Ben said. "No one stole your limo while we were gone."

It was becoming more apparent to Erik that Ben and Troy were very close friends, although they seemed to have quite different characteristics. Ben appeared to be – under normal conditions – an energetic sort, while Troy tended to show the signs of preferring the part of the spectator in the bleachers to that of the athlete on the playing field.

"Limo?" Erik said as he eyed the only other car in sight – the dark blue Mustang that sported an orange hood and front fender, and a pale yellow driver's door.

"Yeah," Ben chuckled. "That magnificent automobile... we call it the limo—"

"Well, you have to admit," Troy interrupted. "It runs like a million bucks... and we had a lot of great times in that car..."

"Yeah, until you let it roll down the hill, sideswipe three fence posts and hit a tree."

"Okay, Ben," Troy said, laughing a little, too. "You don't have to rub it in."

"Anyway," Ben continued. "His dad is getting a new car, and Troy gets his old one, and the limo is for sale. But I doubt anyone will want it, now."

"Why? Is it jizzicked?" Erik asked.

"Is it *what?*"

"Jizzicked... you know... ruined beyond repair. Don't you

guys understand plain English?"

Ben glanced at Troy. "Another Maine thing."

"It just looks like hell, that's all," Troy said. "Hey, Ben. How come you left the lights on in the house?"

"Bryan's here. He's probably watching TV."

The inside of the older house had been remodeled, but still retained a "country" look – knotty pine walls and exposed log ceiling beams, with an old wooden wagon wheel supporting several old-fashioned oil lamps converted to electric bulbs as the living room overhead light. Erik was quite impressed with the surprising appearance. But it wasn't difficult to determine that a bachelor lived there, and he wasn't the best housekeeper.

"Welcome to my mess," Ben said as they came into the living room. A few stray clothes draped over the backs of chairs. Books, magazines and newspapers were in unruly stacks, but conveniently located within easy reach of the recliner and sofa. A pizza box and a couple of empty Coke cans nicely decorated the coffee table. Plates, cups, glasses and silverware had been left here and there, and the carpet looked as though it hadn't seen a vacuum in the past decade.

On one end of the couch, in a casual but comfortable-looking slump, apparently sound asleep and unaware of the others around him, sat another young fellow bearing remarkable resemblance to Ben. Erik quickly surmised that this must be the Bryan mentioned earlier, and he must be Ben's brother.

Troy didn't need an invitation to make himself at home; he headed straight for his favorite spot on the other end of the couch, gently wrestled the TV remote from Bryan's limp hand, pointed it toward the TV and switched it off – he obviously spent a lot of time here.

"Have a seat," Ben offered Erik. "And that's my brother, Bryan," he said, nodding to the snoring lad on the couch. He gathered up the pizza box and cans and relocated them to the kitchen table.

"Nice place," Erik commented, despite the lack of any housekeeping. Well, it would be nice, he thought, if it were straightened up a bit.

"Thanks," Ben replied. "I guess it needs a good cleaning …
and I'm not very good at that." He glanced around the room as
if he were reminiscing. "Dad helped me remodel it a couple
summers ago. Wonder if he'll ever see it again."

Erik didn't think he was qualified, yet, to start asking any questions. He would wait for the information to come to him.

The commotion aroused the sleeping Bryan. He slowly
opened his eyes, stretched his arms over his head, yawned, and
squinted toward the clock. "When did you guys get here?" he
mumbled amidst another yawn. Then he noticed the stranger
sitting in the recliner.

"Just a little while ago," Troy replied.

"Did Sleeping Beauty wake up?" Ben called from the kitchen.
He'd made another trip with a few dishes collected from around
the room.

"I couldn't help it," Bryan whined. "I was tired."

Ben came back into the room. "This is Erik. He's gonna stay
here for a while."

"In the spare room?"

"Well, I'm not gonna make him sleep in the back yard, you
numbskull."

"Cool," Bryan said. "Hey, Ben. Can you give me a ride
home?"

"Why don't you stay here tonight?"

"Cause some friends are picking me up early in the morning.
We're going to a Brewers game in Milwaukee."

"Oh, all right. Let's go." Ben turned to Troy. "I'll be right
back."

"See ya later, Troy," Bryan said. "And I guess I'll see you
again sometime, too," he told Erik. He and Ben hiked out the
door.

"He seems like a nice guy," Erik said after the brothers had
left.

"Bryan? He's okay, but he can get a little crazy sometimes."

"How do you mean?"

"Bryan's eighteen, goin' on twelve. He just graduated, and
he's always tryin' to live up to his brother's reputation, but he

couldn't ever be quite as good as Ben."

"Good at what?"

"Sports... wrestling, mainly. Ben won two State Championships his junior and senior years. No one in this school has ever
done that before. Bryan's good, but not *that* good."

Erik's eyes lit up. He had been a wrestler in high school, too –
even won a regional tournament once, but he never went to State.
At least, he had something in common with Ben.

"Their folks divorced about three or four years ago," Troy
went on. "Bryan lives with his mom, but Ben has always felt a
little resentment toward her for leaving his dad, so he doesn't visit her very much. But Bryan comes over here quite often and
stays with Ben. He's even got his own room upstairs."

"You two are pretty close, aren't ya?"

"Closer than brothers, probably," Troy said. "We grew up
together living next door to each other. I have twin sisters – ten
years older – and so there wasn't ever much goin' on at our house
that interested me, and I spent a lot of time at the Hudsons'
house."

"So... what happened to Ben's father?" Erik asked.

"He disappeared a little over a month ago – just vanished.
Went to his office one day, and hasn't been seen since."

"Office? What kind of office?"

"Stanley owned a trucking company – Hudson Trucking – had
fifteen trucks until Peter Barrington came along. I guess he
bought into the company and became a partner... about five
years ago... and the size of the company doubled. He had another trucking outfit in Chicago, and they combined the two, but
they still called it Hudson. I worked for Stan during the summers, washing trucks and running errands and stuff like that, but
now that he's gone, so am I."

"Have the police been looking for him?"

"Oh... yeah... they went through the motions for a while, but
you could've whistled down the vent pipe to hell for all the good
it did. When Ben came home from Colorado this spring, all they
told him was that there was no evidence of foul play, and there
wasn't any more they could do."

"Colorado? What was Ben doing in Colorado?"

"College. He's been out there two years at the University in Fort Collins... Civil Engineering."

Now it made more sense to Erik why he had been impressed with Ben right from the very start. He knew that it must take a pretty smart guy to manage engineering school, and being a State Wrestling Champion meant he could manage himself pretty well, too. But he was a lousy housekeeper, although, considering the current state of affairs, it might explain the messy house.

The sound of Ben's pickup drifted in through the screen door, and a couple of minutes later Ben plopped down on the couch beside Troy. "Sorry 'bout that," he said to Erik. "Don't know why he waited 'til now to tell me he needed a ride."

Erik just smiled and shrugged his shoulders.

"Well, now that you've seen the place," Ben said, "D'ya think you wanna stay here?"

"Sure," Erik responded quickly. "How much is it gonna cost me?"

"Nothing," Ben said. "That is, if you'll help clean up the place a little."

Erik glanced around. Cleaning this place would be like sweeping Main Street with a toothbrush. But if that's all it would cost him for a place to live, he was willing to give it a try. "That sounds like a deal to me."

"And then, after a while," Ben added, "maybe we can figure out a way to get you a job working for Barrington."

Now Erik understood a little better why Ben was being so generous and friendly. It had finally come out. He wanted a spy. "And how do you figure I'm gonna be able to help you?"

"Well, 'cause you're new here. He doesn't know you. You might be able to get places and hear things."

"Yeah," Troy interrupted. "Maybe he could get my old job. I don't think he's ever hired anyone to replace me."

"But, what about my job at Bert Greer's place?"

"It would only be part time, you can be sure," Ben said. "And didn't you say it was part time at Bert's, too?"

"Well, yeah... but isn't this guy... Barrington... your dad's business partner? Can't you just talk to him?"

Ben leaned forward on the couch. "I've tried, but he's hiding something from me. Bryan got the same treatment."

"He and your dad are friends, aren't they? I mean... they *are* partners."

"Well, Erik, it's like this." Ben settled back on the couch. "My dad started out a long time ago with one little truck, hauling live-stock to the sales barn for area farmers. The business grew, and a few years ago his fleet was fifteen over-the-road tractor-trailer rigs, and he was quite successful. He's one of those guys who always seem to make things happen in his favor, and he's always kept us fed... and then some.

"But then operating costs started getting out of control, and it was cuttin' into the profits. So Dad decided to go into partner-ship with this guy from Chicago... he thought getting bigger could compensate."

"Was that guy Barrington?" Erik asked.

"Yep. Dad and Peter had been helping each other out with backhauls for several years, and they worked out a deal that seemed like a good arrangement. Peter moved his whole opera-tion out of Chicago, except for a brokerage office so they could keep all their local customers in that area. They built a new shop and warehouse, and operated the business from here."

"So..." Erik said. "Something must've gone wrong."

"Wrong?" Ben replied. It seemed as if talking about the sub-ject caused him great pain. "Nothing went right! Peter had these hotshot crooked lawyers and accountants in Chicago and they started doctoring the books. Dad found out about it, and when he threatened to dissolve the partnership, Peter straightened up his act."

"Until now?"

"Yeah. I think Dad suspected trouble last winter when Peter started negotiating with some foreigners, and all the regular cus-tomers weren't getting the service they were used to getting."

"So... what happened?"

"Well, I don't know for sure. I was in Colorado at school for two years, and now, none of the drivers who worked for Dad are here anymore."

"Why?"

"They didn't like Peter and the way he was doing business. They all quit. Now all the drivers are strangers from Chicago."

Erik sat up straight. He knew he wasn't very knowledgeable about big trucks or the business they involved. Ben and his bro-ken family – and the people they associated with – seemed somewhat rough around the edges. And the way this house looked, Erik wondered if he was getting in over his head.

On the other hand, Ben attended an expensive college, wore modest but nice clothes, drove a late model four-wheel-drive pick up, and he had a nice home – all the things in life that pointed toward success and money. His best friend, Troy, was clean-cut and seemed to have a heart of gold – not the kind of person who would hang out with a deadbeat. But Erik still had some doubts.

"So, what do you plan to do next?" He still didn't like the idea of infiltrating a business run by a man who sounded like a dangerous criminal.

"Well, I think there's more to all this than meets the eye. I've talked to the Police Chief and the County Sheriff. They're convinced that Barrington hasn't done anything wrong, and they haven't found anything that indicates foul play. They've all but told me that there's nothing more they can do. So, I guess I'm on my own."

After the first two or three difficult days of feeling each other out as people, Ben and Erik began forming a relationship based on mutual respect for each other. It was necessary as roommates. Although their cultures were slightly different, they had a lot in common, and they both had a lively interest in the world around them.

Ben had always been a creature of regular habits. He liked getting up at a certain early hour, work out for a certain period of time, eat and drink on schedule, see his friends daily and his enemies only when an interrupted schedule made it absolutely necessary to be irritable with someone, which was a rare occasion. Periodically the pressure of circumstances forced him to alter his schedule, but he quickly settled into the new one and adjusted remarkably with a minimum of discomfort. His approach to this was always casual, never trying to impose himself on life, but rather fitting quietly into it like tired feet into a comfortable pair of old shoes.

He rarely thought about the past, even though his accomplishments as a young athlete were commendable. But the past was there, of course, lurking uninhibited in the shadows of his memory, and occasionally, spurred by some vivid, instantly recognizable image, it would rush out to overwhelm him. Now, though, his memories were mostly of his father.

Tuesday June 26

In a week's time, Ben had heard nothing from Sheriff Lowery. He started calling every day, hopeful of hearing some news. Finally the sheriff told him to come into the office for a little chat. Ben wasn't sure whether that meant good news or bad; he had to be ready for either.   He settled into the chair the sheriff offered and patiently waited while he finished a phone conversation.

"Okay, Ben," Lowery said, looking back and forth from Ben and a stack of papers on his desk as if determining what should be next on his list of priorities. "How are you this morning?"

"Okay, I guess. I hope you have some news about my dad."

"Well, Ben, you know we're doing everything we can. We've checked out Peter Barrington's background more thoroughly."

Ben squirmed in his chair and stared across the desk at the papers.

"Quite frankly, Ben, I don't see anything to support your suspicions." The lawman scanned over a few pages of notes and continued. "His father was a cop in Chicago. The family moved to Downer's Grove after Peter's older brother was shot and killed in a bungled gas station hold-up. Peter was ten years old at the time.

"At Downer's Grove Peter was enrolled at St. Joseph's Catholic School. His grades were above average; he was a star on their baseball team; he even worked as an assistant to the parish priest and served as an altar boy."

Ben listened, but he couldn't understand what any of this had to do with the current-day Peter Barrington.

Lowery went on. "When Peter graduated from high school in 1965, he took a job as office boy and stockroom clerk at a construction company. About a year later he went to work for Western Union and eventually became a branch manager.

"Then a few years after that he gradually started buying into several small businesses, one of which is the cartage company that he combined with Hudson Trucking five years ago."

Ben shook his head and stared at the sheriff who appeared that he was finished with his report of findings. "Is that all? What about the bookmaking racket he ran while he worked for Western Union? What about all the shady stuff he pulled with his crooked lawyers and accountants? Did you find out any of that stuff?"

The sheriff responded with a startled expression. "There's nothing on his police record, Ben. Where are you getting that kind of information?"

"From my dad. These are things that he found out or that Peter told him."

"And do you believe that to be fact? Or maybe it could be just a big shot bragging up a little exaggeration?"

"No. I've been around Peter enough to know that it's probably not exaggeration."

"Well, I've spent some time with him, too, and he seems like a well-behaved businessman."

"Of course he's going to be on his best behavior when you're around. I know Peter better than that. I don't trust him."

Sheriff Lowery tossed the papers on the desk and leaned back in his chair, folding his arms across his chest. "Ben, I can understand that you're upset about your father disappearing, but I also think that you're being a little too harsh with Peter. He has merely taken steps to protect himself and the business. Your dad would've done the same if the tables were turned."

It appeared to Ben that he was getting nowhere with this conversation. "Are you telling me that you're going to quit looking?"

"If we happen across any new leads, of course, we'll look into them. But for right now, Ben, there just isn't anything to follow."

Friday June 29

It was early evening when Ben heard a car door slam out in the driveway. He thought it might be Erik arriving home a little earlier than planned. As the car sped away he looked out the window to see Bryan sauntering toward the front door.

"Mom went shopping with some other women and they were going to have dinner in La Crosse. Mind if I stay here and eat with you?"

Ben nodded his approval. "I'm thawing out some hamburger, so it'll be a little while before we eat. And there's nobody else here tonight, either."

"Where's Erik?"

"Working late."

"Troy?"

"Out with Mandy."

They sat on the couch in silence watching the TV news. Ben thought this might be Bryan's attempt to present the Florida move. So far, he had said nothing about it, and Ben decided it was time to confront the issue. "So, what have you decided on the move to Florida?"

"How did you know about that?"

"Mom told me... the day I talked to her when I first got back."

"Bryan sank down into the couch as if he were trying to hide. "She told me not to say anything to anybody until she knew for sure."

"Well it definitely sounded to me like a sure thing. She told me the date she starts her new job. Have you even given this any thought?"

"I don't know what to think."

"D'ya wanna talk about it?"

Bryan gestured indecisively with a shoulder shrug.

"Look, Bryan," Ben said. "You're eighteen years old. You

need to start thinking for yourself... about what you want to do with your life. What about school? Have you thought about that?"

"Sure, I've thought about it."

"And?"

"And it's probably not gonna happen... not right now."

"Why do you say that?"

"Well, every time I bring up the subject to Mom she brushes it off like it was dandruff."

"Why are you relying on her?"

"Real easy for you to say that! Dad already got you half-way through."

"Yeah, he's helped me, but I've been working all the time, too."

"Face the reality, Ben. I'm not getting that help. Dad ain't comin' back."

"I wish you'd stop being so negative about that. And what are you saying? That you're just going to give up everything here and go to Florida?"

"Seems like that's what Mom is doing."

"She's going because of a career. She's a real estate agent, and it's probably a good opportunity for her. What reason do you have?"

"It's like this, Ben." Bryan hesitated a moment. "I turned out to be a big disappointment to everybody 'cause I wasn't as good a wrestler as you. Dad gave you this house, and he paid for your college. What's he given me? Maybe I just want to see what Florida has to offer."

"Being a good wrestler has nothing to do with it, you bone-head." Ben put his arm across his brother's shoulders. "Dad put away some emergency money that I have access to, and I've been saving quite a bit from my job in Colorado. If you want to go to school, I'll help you get through the first year. It's what Dad would want."

"But, what about your school?"

"Don't worry about me. I can take care of myself."

Bryan leaned forward with elbows on knees. "I don't know, Ben. I'll have to think about it."

Monday July 16, 2001

Nearly a month had gone by since Erik Wilson landed on
Wisconsin soil and had decided to take his chances on a lifestyle
quite different than he had expected to find. Although he had
little opportunity to spend much time with Ben, Erik diligently
fulfilled his obligation to clean the house from top to bottom in
return for his free accommodations. It had been quite a task, and
he was thankful that Bryan had spent a lot of time at the house
while Ben searched far and wide for their missing father.   His
companionship diverted the loneliness that might have taken its
toll on Erik in this unfamiliar country, and in a town so far away
from home where he knew hardly anyone.

But now Bryan was gone. Ben hoped the pep talk to his
brother had helped, and that the decision to go to Florida with
his mother was really his decision and not hers. Laura had de-
clined Ben's help with the move, so it was probably good that she
at least had Bryan there to help her settle into a new home in
Tampa. And unless Bryan experienced a severe case of home-
sickness, Ben was quite certain that he would choose the sunny
Florida lifestyle.

Bert Greer's used car business was booming, and he was giving Erik all the work he wanted. Chet, the full-time mechanic,
was teaching him a lot beyond the skills he had attained from his
high school shop courses, and Bert seemed satisfied with his per-
formance. Erik was beginning to feel good about himself again.

Spending a good share of his time with Chet in the shop, he
was getting to know that Chet was nothing short of a playboy
extraordinaire. Chet always had tales to tell of his exploits at his
favorite hangout – a bar called The Den – where he whiled away
most of his nighttime hours, and where he was known as "Charlie," because of his harem he call his "Angels."   At times, Erik
thought it might be fun to experience some of the Den's social
culture; however, he wasn't of legal age to enter such places. And
he didn't have a car to get there.

He was getting tired of walking to and from work every day,
too. If he was lucky, he might beg a ride from Ben, but the tim-

ing wasn't always right, and he usually walked more than he rode. Bert had attempted to sell him a car from the lot, but even at wholesale price, Erik thought the terms were a little steep for his financial status just yet.

"Why don't you buy the limo from Troy?" Ben suggested one evening during supper.

"Don't know that I can afford to buy any car yet. I'm only taking home two hundred on a good week, ya know."

"He doesn't want much for the limo."

"How much d'ya think?"

"Three or four hundred bucks."

"Are you serious?"

"That's what he told me."

"Guess maybe I could swing a deal like that. How much are tags in Wisconsin?"

"Forty-five."

Erik did some quick calculations in his head, and he decided he should try to make a deal with Troy, but first he'd have a little talk with Bert and Chet about the repairs it would need.

"And remember," Ben added. "It needs a set of tires pretty bad."

"That shouldn't be a problem. I can get used tires from Bert real cheap. I'm more concerned about getting it all one color again."

"Chet should be able to help you with that – he's a pretty good painter."

"Yeah, I guess he is, but how did you know that?"

"Chet worked in my dad's shop."

"That's funny. He's never mentioned that."

"Probably because Dad fired him."

"Why?"

"He spent too much time in the bars... couldn't get anything done 'cause he was hung over half the time."

"He seems to get things done at our shop, and I haven't ever seen him cuttin' the curwhibbles."

"Cutting the *what?*"

"Cuttin' the curwhibbles."

"I suppose that's the *Maineac* way of saying hung over."

"Sort of. I'm glad to see you're starting to learn English."

As for the Mustang, Erik found himself quite charged and eager for another milestone in his new life to become reality. With a car, he would feel less restricted, and more importantly, it was something tangible larger than a backpack that he could call his own. It probably wasn't the greatest car in the world – but it would be *his* car. He had been dreaming of this day, but he never thought it would come this soon. Visions scooted around in his head as he imagined himself arriving at work every day in his own car, and cruising through the countryside with the wind blowing in his hair. It was a new feeling of freedom.

His anxiety built as the minutes ticked by. He decided that he didn't want to wait until tomorrow to talk to Bert and Chet – they might try to convince him to buy a more expensive car from Bert's lot. No. He had to talk to Troy tonight. He went to the phone and dialed the number.

A few minutes later, he returned to the kitchen table where Ben was scanning the current issue of the *Times*.

"So, what'd he say?" Ben asked, not looking up from the local news.

"He's coming over with the title. And he said you have a set of keys here."

Ben looked up to see Erik's anxious and elated expression. "Sounds like you bought a car."

"Yeah! Ain't it great?"

"I think the keys are in that top drawer by the refrigerator." Ben was glad for Erik, but he didn't show any outward signs of it. Nothing seemed to make him happy.

Erik found the keys and headed out the door. The Mustang had been parked along side the garage in the grass two weeks ago, and already the grass had grown up around it, as if it were abandoned and forgotten. In a way, it had been, as Troy hadn't given it much thought since his dad had turned over the Buick Regal to him. But now, the Mustang – the "limo" – would be resurrected back to usefulness.

It sputtered and coughed a little at first, but after a few seconds, the motor ran smoothly. Erik put the shift lever in low gear and eased the car out of the grass and onto the driveway in front of the garage. He had never taken a close look at it before now, but even though it was a rather old car, it didn't seem all that bad – Troy had kept it clean, at least. Erik's talents, with a little help and advice from Chet, would get it back into shape in no time.

Troy's shiny, black Buick Regal pulled into the driveway and stopped next to the Mustang.

"So, what d'ya think?" Troy said, peering through the open driver's door window of the limo. Erik studied the instrument panel and replied, "I think we should take her for a little spin."

Troy got in the passenger seat. "What's the gas gauge read?"

"It says full."

"Okay. Let's go." He pulled the door shut and explained to Erik about the gas gauge not being all that reliable, as it would read full for a long time, then abruptly fall to below a quarter, and when it did that, he should be looking for a gas station real soon.

Erik eased down the driveway, turned onto the road into town, and took the Mustang up to a moderate speed. It seemed to run and drive quite well for an old car with over a hundred thousand miles on the odometer. He noticed a couple of little rattles, but he certainly wasn't about to complain. After a little jaunt around town, Erik pointed the limo back toward home. As he parked in front of the garage door again, Troy asked, "Ben in the house?"

Erik nodded. "He was reading the paper when I left."

"Good. I have to talk to him. And I'll bring the title for the Mustang in with me."

"I'll be right behind you."

Ben still sat at the kitchen table with the newspaper spread out in front of him, but his gaze was off somewhere in another world unknown to anyone but him. Erik and Troy sat down across from him, and Troy produced an envelope containing the car title that he handed to Erik.

"Hey, Ben. Guess what," Troy said.

Ben broke his trance-like stare at the wall and turned to Troy, but he didn't utter a word.

"Dad said I can transfer to Fort Collins this fall if I want to."

Ben's blank expression turned to a frown. "But I'm not going back to Colorado."

"But I thought you had a good job out there, too."

"That's not the point. I'm not going back until I know what has happened to Dad. I thought you would figure that out."

"Sorry... I wasn't thinking about that."

Wanting to quickly change the subject, Ben said, "I hear you sold the limo to Erik."

Erik had the title unfolded, lying in front of him on the table. It had been signed by the seller and was ready for the transfer. "What do I do with this, now?"

"You take it to the Motor Vehicle office in La Crosse," Ben explained, "... pay for the transfer fee, sales tax, and new plates, and they give you a new title with your name on it."

"Well, I don't know where to find anything in La Crosse," Erik responded. "Will you go with me?"

"Sure. We can go tomorrow morning if you want. There and back... should take about two hours."

"Okay. I'll call Bert and tell him I'll be in later than usual." Erik trotted off, and a little while later, returned to hand Troy three crisp hundred dollar bills.

Tuesday July 17

Erik returned to the shop by 11 o'clock after Ben and Troy had escorted him to the Motor Vehicle Department. Chet was standing at the back door with a cup of coffee and a cigarette when Erik pulled into the back lot and parked the Mustang that now legally belonged to him. "So, you bought the limo, eh?" he said, as Erik strutted across the lot.

"Yeah," Erik responded proudly. "And I'm hoping you can help me get it all one color again." He wondered why Chet knew the Mustang was affectionately called the "limo," but then he remembered the connection: Hudson Trucking Company – he used to work there, as did Troy.

"One color?" Chet said. "I think you should leave it multi-colored. It adds character," he joked.

Erik chuckled a little, even though he failed to see any amusement in Chet's sarcasm.

"Well, then, as long as you're at it, I know some people from Chicago who can get you chrome rims, or just about anything you want – real cheap."

"That's okay," Erik replied. "I'll be happy just to get it all blue again. So, will you show me what to do? I know you're a good painter." He thought tossing in a little compliment might increase his odds.

"Well, I s'pose so. Ask Bert if he'll let you use the shop after hours. I'd say we could knock this out in two or three nights."

"Great! I'll talk to him this afternoon."

When he came home after work that day, Erik found Ben sitting alone on the back deck and excitedly told him the good news about restoring the Mustang to its original color, and that Chet would help him with the painting project. But it was easy to see that Ben didn't share his excitement. He just smiled and nodded acknowledgement.

After returning from the trip to La Crosse, Ben had spent most of the day reminiscing and attempting to put everything in perspective as to move forward with his life. For the first time since he came home from Colorado he understood how much he had changed. The house, it seemed, was a kind of measuring stick. It had belonged to the Ben who went off to see the world, to acquire a new sense of values and judgment. A crude, half-developed boy had gone away, and an educated man had come back.

Out of all he had learned in the lecture halls, classrooms, and labs, and from the contacts with people whose very lives were steeped in tradition, he was aware of a few things in his character and feelings that remained unchanged. One was his love for this part of the Midwest with its great rolling hills and valleys, its forests, streams and lakes. He had learned to like Colorado, too, with its grand mountains and magnificent sunrises and sunsets. Fort Collins had become more to him than just a showy college town, and in a way he loved even the monstrosity of man's encroachment upon the wilderness, and the promise of a future. But Wisconsin was still his home.

The other thing that remained was his respect and feelings for his father. If they had changed at all, they had risen to a higher level. He knew now, as he had always known, that Stanley Hudson was a great man, and that this quality would be recognized anywhere in the world, in any society, as it was recognized in his hometown. He was among those who were spoken of with respect. He had established his position with rocklike security and maintained dignity for his family. It was painfully difficult to imagine that anyone could have done harm to such a good man.

It had seemed odd to Ben that his father's house on the other side of town appeared unmolested, and without any signs of investigation. He had expected to see the yellow police ribbons surrounding the premises and blocking the doors. But there had been none. Even the company pickup truck that his dad always drove, found abandoned, had been returned to the driveway instead of being impounded by the police. It certainly was a puzzling circumstance.

"Would you like to go for a little ride?" Ben asked Erik who had settled down in a chair beside him.

"Where to?" Erik said.

"I wanna check out our old shop. It's only a couple of miles."

"Sure," Erik agreed. "Let me change my clothes first."

They went in Ben's truck into the country across town to the shop – small in comparison to the new one – where Stan Hudson had built his business before Peter Barrington became a partner.

"This is where Dad started," Ben explained as they walked around the old cement block structure. He gazed at the peeled white paint, remembering the entire summer it had taken him as a boy of twelve to brush paint that whole building, and how proud he was when it was finished.

This was the last spot where Stan Hudson was known to be. And now, once again, it seemed unusual that nothing was protecting the scene of the crime – if there had been a crime committed.

As they approached the front door, Ben dug a key out of his pocket. He unlocked the door and they went in. Since the shop was barely large enough to accommodate one truck, the tiny office space hardly adequate for the growing business, and the available land too small for the necessary expansion, this building had been relegated to storage space. But it belonged solely to Stan Hudson, so Ben felt totally justified entering the property. He hadn't been in there since last summer, but the contents had changed very little. Stacks of truck tires, a spare diesel engine, and various truck parts occupied the garage area, and the old wooden desk and chairs in the office held a generous layer of dust. Actually, nothing had been removed because the new office had warranted all new furniture. Except for the dusty loneliness, it looked about the same as it had years ago.

Ben wandered around the shop, gazing over all the things that remained. In the dim light, Erik could see all the unanswered questions in his friend's face. "Did you expect to find something here?" he asked.

"No, I didn't expect to find anything here – well, put it this way. I'm hoping for a hunch."

"You mean you think a ghost will come along and tell you where to look?"

"No. But I do think, though, that being here where it all started, maybe a hunch will come to me."

"Guess I'm not exactly following what you're getting at."

"It's that sudden feeling that you just know. Like an old phonograph record – it gives back the sounds made long ago. An event made an impression on that record, and it remains there to be heard later. Maybe it's the same with a knife or a gun or a chair – maybe there's a message left on it by the energy from the person who handled it. You touch the thing, and maybe the energy and the message comes to you."

Erik wondered if it were possible that seeing the old building and touching the relics of the past would render any clues – or hunches, like Ben was suggesting. He was quite sure the idea was nonsense, but it was certainly interesting nonsense.

Saturday July 21

At the moment when the shot rang out, Erik Wilson was sitting alone on a large rock at the dark edge of the parking lot behind the truck stop, contemplating his options, as the restaurant
was closed. The sound at this hour – it was well past eleven
o'clock – was so unexpected that for a few moments he continued to sit in a kind of dazed astonishment. He thought it might
have been a firecracker, but it had that certain snap of a small caliber gun. Then the patter of feet running across the gravel made
him turn his head sharply. He could see someone racing toward
the lot from the vicinity of another square building, and a short
distance behind him ran several others.

As the figure being chased came nearer, Erik stood up, trying
to get a better look. The pursued man was putting some distance
between him and his adversaries, but just as he crossed a narrow
strip of grass, he tripped and fell. Before he could recover, Erik
counted four others upon him. It was at that moment that Erik's
instincts drew him to the fallen man's aid. He didn't particularly
like street fighting, and he disliked more the uneven odds of this
spectacle. He darted toward the skirmish, and in the cover of
darkness his approach presented an element of surprise, affording
him a slight advantage.

There was no doubt about the surprise – if a tornado had descended over the heads of the four, they could hardly have been
more astonished. One of the ruffians had a knee on the downed
man's stomach, about to deliver a disabling blow when a strong
arm seized him around his neck from behind, another grip on the
seat of his pants, and he was flung sideways into one of his
friends, who in turn, completely lost his balance and cannoned
headlong into the third. They all tumbled over a slight embankment into a tangled heap. They had not expected to encounter
the likes of an accomplished wrestler.

Erik turned just in time to meet the rush of the fourth man.
One quick glance was enough to convince Erik that he was no
match for a man that seemed twice his size, so he dived like a
bolt of lightning for the large man's legs. The man's head met

the ground with a crack, and for a time his interest in the proceedings was minimal, allowing Erik a long moment to assess the situation.

The victim had regained his feet. Erik only had a brief glimpse of him charging his assailants like an enraged bull, for just as suddenly he became aware of another movement to his other side. Perhaps it was the glint of what Erik thought was a knife blade that caught his eye. Creeping toward him was a slight man, but now there was no doubt in Erik's mind about the weapon. Even though the attacker realized Erik's awareness of his stealth approach, he did not cease his strange, catlike advance.

Erik's keen eyes sensed that unmistakable warning of a frantic movement. He stepped quickly to the side just as the knifeman committed to a forward lunge. The knife made a harmless sweep through the air, and before the man could recover, Erik's hands were latched to his arm, and with one fast jerk and twist, he heard a snap followed by a yelp of pain. The knife fell to the ground, and Erik, stepping back, delivered a left jab to the jaw. The attacker flopped over and hit the ground like a sack of flour.

Erik stooped down to pick up the knife, and as he straightened up, he noticed the victim of the assault coming toward him. He had apparently been successful in driving away the others.

"Ben?" Erik gasped. "Is that you?"

"Yeah," came the reply. "Who'd you expect?"

"Are you hurt?"

"No... just some bruises... I think. How 'bout you?"

"Not a scratch, but I think I broke this guy's arm."

"Broke his arm? Too bad it wasn't his head." Ben glanced quickly around. "C'mon... let's get out of here."

"I'm working on the Mustang down at the shop. We can get out of sight there." Erik tossed the knife into the weeds as he led the way along the backside of the lot toward the used car shop.

"What were you doing there?" Ben asked. "Not that I wasn't glad you were."

"Just decided to take a little break and go for a walk."

"Those dirty swine."

"S'pose they'll come back?"

"No… I'm sure they've had their bellyful for one night."

Half an hour later, cleaned up into some resemblance of re-spectability, and with a small plastic bandage strip pasted to his forehead, Ben sat on a step stool admiring the Mustang while Erik put away his tools.   "Looks better than it did," he com-mented.

Thanks to Mr. Greer for allowing Erik to use the shop, the Mustang was all one color again. The blue on the hood, left front fender, and driver's side door didn't match the rest of the car ex-actly, but it was quite an improvement over the orange and yellow junkyard replacement parts. Erik had stripped off all the masking tape and paper, but the new paint wasn't dry enough to take out into any dust or bugs that night.

Erik was intensely curious about the men that had assaulted Ben, but Ben wasn't offering much. He had suspicions that they were somehow connected to the disappearance of Ben's father, and the strange operation of the trucking company that should rightfully belong to Ben, if it were determined that Ben's father was deceased. He sincerely hoped that wasn't the case, but he feared that Ben was slowly losing faith. Finally, Erik asked, "Who were those guys? And why did they come after you?"

"They're Barrington's men, and I'd guess they want to make sure I don't get in their way."

"In the way?"

"You see… they didn't expect me to be back here to inter-fere…"

"Interfere with what?"

"Barrington has pretty much taken over Dad's company, and he told me that because he had paid off Dad's debts, there wasn't anything left for me. Then he showed me papers that Dad had signed his share of the business over to Barrington before he dis-appeared, but I'm quite sure those papers are forgeries. My dad wouldn't have done that. He would have faced his problems, even if he was broke, which he wasn't. And he wouldn't have run away."

"So, how did it happen that you got tangled up with Barring-ton's thugs tonight?"

"I was driving by the warehouse, and I saw some lights on. That seemed a little unusual for this time of night. Then I recognized a couple of the cars, so I parked my truck down the road and snuck over there to see what was goin' on. Sure enough, they were all in there having a powwow. Guess I must've made some noise that I shouldn't have, and when I realized they had discovered me there, I didn't get away quick enough."

"I heard a gunshot," Erik said.

"That was Lenny King. I think he's kinda the ringleader. But he didn't join in on the chase. At least I didn't see him with the ones we were fighting."

"Shouldn't we go to the cops about this?"

"They won't do anything. I think Barrington has the sheriff in his back pocket."

Monday July 30

Ben stayed out of sight, going out in public only if he had to. Troy and Erik went about business as usual, although Erik constantly kept one eye on the lookout for the men with whom he and Ben had had the encounter. He couldn't help but think that it had been an attempt on Ben's life, but Ben had insisted on keeping it quiet. Erik wasn't sure that he'd recognize any of the men again, or if they'd recognize him, but he still kept conscious of the possibility that they might.

They occupied a table at the very far end of the truck stop dining room where they could survey nearly the entire place, yet remain inconspicuous to the rest of the crowd. Their pitcher of coffee nearly gone, and the usual mountain of empty sugar packets piled in front of Troy, Erik stared coldly at four men sitting in a booth at the opposite end of the room. One of them, Erik was quite certain, was a member of the team that had assaulted Ben. His dark features were very distinctive, and when he glanced to the other side of the room, he acted as if he had recognized Erik. Another man Erik thought to be in his late 40s, and another dark complexioned man with much the same features as the first sat at the table, and they seemed to be in a very serious conversation.

"Troy. Do you know those men?" Erik nodded toward them.

Troy stared for just a short while. "The older fellow is Peter Barrington. The others are Lenny King, Jimmy Belmont, and Sid Hollister. They all work for Barrington. Lenny and Jimmy are drivers he brought in from Chicago; Sid is the mechanic in the shop. I never got to know any of them very well."

Another man walked in and sat down at their table. "That's John Wolf... another one of Barrington's drivers," Troy added.

Erik could just barely hear him tell the others that "Drake wanted them to come down." Hearing that, all four men got up to leave.

"Who's Drake?" Erik whispered.

"Don't know."

"Well, we're gonna follow 'em. C'mon."

The sun had dipped below the western horizon a half-hour ago, and now the night was closing in. While Troy paid for the coffee, Erik watched discretely as three of the men got into a silver Mercedes sedan and headed toward the highway. Barrington had departed in the other direction in his white Suburban. Within seconds, Erik and Troy were in the Mustang and in pursuit of the Mercedes, just far enough behind as not to be noticed. After they had turned onto Highway 56 at Viroqua, Erik asked, "Where are they headed?"

"Well, this road goes to the river."

"The Mississippi?"

"Yep. It's about twenty miles to Genoa."

At Genoa they passed by a large, old-looking, tin-sided warehouse. Erik gazed beyond it, out in the river, where lights from several houseboats gleamed as the moonlight danced on the silvery water around them. "Is that the Mississippi?" he asked. He had never seen it before.

"That it is," replied Troy.

They had driven some distance on the Great River Road. It seemed like a different world to Erik and he hoped he would have the chance to see it sometime in the daylight.

The Mercedes' brake lights came on and the vehicle veered off to the left into a driveway shrouded with tall trees. So they wouldn't appear conspicuous, Erik drove on past the end of the driveway. Troy spotted the name "Ed Drake" on the mailbox.

Several cars and pickups were parked in the grass on the river side of the highway. "We can park there... people fishing," Troy suggested. Erik pulled in behind them, about a hundred yards from the driveway.

As they walked briskly toward the Drake driveway, staying well off the roadway in the grass, Troy asked, "What do you expect to find here?"

"We might find out something about Ben's father."

"Like what?"

"Well, where he went... what happened to him."

"But that was a long time ago."

"Maybe if we can find out what these bastards are up to now, it might be a clue to what happened to Ben's dad. Just stay out of sight, and we'll try to listen at a window."

In silence they continued on the dirt road into the darkness created by the thick growth of trees lining both sides of the drive. Occasionally, a shaft of moonlight filtered through from above, and now and then they caught a glimpse of the shimmering water to the right. The leaves rustled in a faint breeze blowing in from the river.

Quite some distance from the highway, the trees parted into an open clearing, and they could see dim light at a couple of windows apparently covered with heavy curtains. To one side was the unmistakable silhouette of the Mercedes they had followed.

With more caution, now, they advanced, leaving the narrow lane and darting from tree trunk to tree trunk. There in the moonlit open spaces, Erik realized that they could probably be seen by anyone watching from the house, but it was a chance they would have to take. Slowly they made their way along the edge of the clearing to where they were only a few feet from the corner of the rambling house built into the hillside. A veranda across the front supported by posts gave the appearance that the house was on stilts.

The sound of voices drifted out to them in the otherwise quiet night air. Erik stood perfectly silent, but the muffled words didn't make any sense.

"Maybe if we get under the deck," Troy suggested in a barely audible whisper, "we might be able to hear more."

Erik nodded, moved cautiously through the shadows to the end pillars and quickly ducked into the blackness beneath the broad veranda floor. Troy followed.

Again the murmur of voices continued among laughter and clinking glasses. There were two voices distinctly conversing in some Arabic language, and at least three or four more speaking English, but only a word or two now and then were distinguishable. Erik caught the words "money," "New York," "boat," "river," "island," but what could any of that mean? The voices trailed off again to a low rumble. Troy grabbed Erik's arm and whispered frantically, "They're coming out!"

Erik looked up to see feet and shadowy figures through the cracks between the veranda floorboards moving toward the stairs leading down to the Mercedes. "We've gotta get out of here," Erik whispered and gestured to the other end of the veranda. Their only escape route, now, was making a mad dash for the woods before any of the men reached the bottom of the steps. When Erik was well within the cover of the trees, he stopped and turned to make sure Troy was still behind him. He wasn't. Then he heard the hum of a motor and saw the headlight beams sweep across the dark woods as the car sped down the grade toward the highway. Erik stepped out into the lane. One by one, the lights went out at the house, so he knew someone was still there – Drake, he assumed. He waited in silence, hoping to notice Troy's movement.

"Here I am," Troy called softly, and his silhouette emerged from the trees. They rejoined and started hiking down the long, dark driveway.

"So what did you make of it?" Erik asked. "Did you hear anything that made sense?"

"I heard them say something about an island on the river, and something about shipments from North Carolina."

"What could any of that have to do with Ben's dad?"

Troy thought a moment. "Well, those shipments are probably coming on Hudson trucks, and something they didn't want Stan

Hudson to know about."

Erik stopped abruptly and put his arm out to stop Troy. "Troy? You've been around this from the very start. Tell me the truth... do you think they killed him? Do you think he's dead?"

"I sincerely hope not. Don't ever tell Ben I said this, but yes, I think it's a possibility. People just don't vanish into thin air."

Friday August 3

At the request of his boss, Erik worked late Friday night to shine up a car that Bert had sold and wanted ready for the customer to pick up Saturday morning. He liked working during the late night hours anyway – no one else around to interrupt, and it was much cooler. It was just after midnight when he had turned out all the lights and closed the shop door. Just as he sauntered across the lot to his Mustang, he noticed the white Chevy Suburban towing a pontoon boat on a trailer. There were several people in the car, but in the dark, be couldn't be sure how many or who.

Nothing was open at that hour to grab a bite to eat, so Erik just headed for home. Ben was sprawled out on the couch watching an old John Wayne movie and munching from a huge bowl of popcorn.

"I saw Barrington's Suburban leaving town a while ago with a pontoon boat."

Ben sat up with a startled, puzzled expression.

"Where would he be going with a boat at this time of night?" Erik asked.

"To the river," Ben replied. "But it is kind of a strange hour."

"Suppose it has anything to do with that meeting Troy and I eavesdropped on the other night?"

"It could. Feel like taking a little ride?"

"I'm kinda hungry."

"Here. You can have the rest of this popcorn. We'll take my truck."

By the time Ben got the truck out of the garage, Erik had changed out of his dirty work jeans into clean shorts and T-shirt and grabbed a couple of cans of *Coke* from the refrigerator. He dumped the popcorn into a paper grocery bag and flew out the door to the driveway where Ben was anxiously waiting.

Ben didn't waste any time getting to the highway. Barrington had a half-hour lead, and there were a number of places he might go once he reached the river. "You said the cottage you followed them to the other night was down below the power plant?"

"Yeah, several miles past that. Do you think that's where they're going?"

"No, but I would guess that they'll go to one of the landings near there. We'll just have to figure out which one."

"How many are there?"

"Well, there's one right at Genoa by the old tobacco ware-house, and one behind the power plant, and another one behind the fish hatchery. And that's just for starters."

Erik popped open a *Coke* to wash down the popcorn.

"And you said they talked about an island... what did they say about it?"

"I couldn't make out every word. But how hard could it be to find them on a river island?"

"Erik... you don't seem to quite understand everything about the Mississippi. She's more than three miles wide in places, and some of the islands are big... like hundreds of acres big."

"Wow!" I didn't realize that. So... do people have houses on them?"

"No. Not around here. This whole area from Wabasha, Minnesota clear down to Rock Island, Illinois is a fish and game refuge. I think all the land is owned by the government."

"So, it would be a pretty good place to hide."

"Yeah, if you wanted to hide." Ben paused in a long, deep thought. "I wonder..."

Erik zeroed in on the same idea. "That maybe your dad is on that island?"

Ben pursed his lips and shrugged his shoulders. After another long, thoughtful pause, he spoke in a suspicious tone: "I don't know what those guys are up to, and those foreigners that Barrington is hooked up with sure make me nervous."

Erik recalled the night at the truck stop when he had gotten the first good look at them. "Troy said they work for Barrington."

"Yeah... the ones you saw. But there are others... big money men."

"How do you know that?" Erik asked.

"My dad mentioned in his letters to me something about Barrington making some deal with some foreigners. Dad wasn't much in favor of whatever was going on, and he said that he and Barrington were having arguments over Dad's opposition."

"So, what kind of deal was it?"

"That I don't know. Dad never gave any details in his letters, other than it involved several million dollars, and I was in Fort Collins at school, so I wasn't around then to see what was happening. But it wasn't too long after that..." Ben hesitated, and then continued with a scared tone, "... that he disappeared. I think he might have discovered something he wasn't supposed to, and they might have..."

"Is that when you came home?"

"No, not right away. I didn't know that Dad had disappeared... only that his letters stopped coming. He had been sending me money – more than I really needed – and I had a job in Fort Collins, too, so I had managed to save quite a bit. But then I didn't hear from him for over a month. And then Bryan called me early one morning and told me that Dad had disappeared. I tried calling Peter, but he wouldn't tell me anything... just that Dad wasn't there."

"And by the time you got back, the trail was cold."

"There was no trail at all. The only thing left was a few thousand dollars in a joint bank account that we had for emergencies. Barrington didn't know about it, or he probably would've had that, too."

Erik carefully asked his next question: "Troy mentioned that there were rumors of your father being in financial trouble. Was that true?"

Ben's expression didn't change. "My dad has had some bad luck in the last couple of years, but he certainly wasn't in financial trouble. He couldn't have been sending me all that money while I was in college if he had been broke, now, could he?" Ben stared at the winding road ahead. "I'm afraid, Erik. I'm afraid."

As Erik took in Ben's drawn features, the fixation of his gaze, and the twitching fingers, he was submerged in a wave of compassion for his friend who was fighting in the dark against odds. Deep within, Erik felt a new sense of friendship stir, and all doubts about Ben vanished.

"Listen, Ben," he said as he put a hand on Ben's shoulder. "It sounds like we're up against something that's bigger than both of us. But I want you to know that I'm with you in this heart and soul. Anything I can do – any way I can help – I will."

Ben turned toward his passenger, and in the dim glow from the instrument panel Erik detected a bit of a smile. "Thanks, my friend," Ben said softly.

They were at the bottom of the steep hill where the road came winding down the bluff into the river valley, and approaching the village of Genoa. The boat landing there would be in plain sight from the River Road. "I doubt they would launch there," Ben said thoughtfully.

"Why not?"

"It's above the locks, and all the big islands are below."

Not a single car, truck or boat trailer occupied the lot at the Genoa landing as they sped by. "We'll check the one at the power plant," Ben said. "But we'll have to walk a little ways. That parking lot is out in the open. They'll see us coming."

Then, as if he'd had an afterthought, Ben turned off the highway abruptly and headed back into the little town. "There's one place I want to check out first," Ben said. "Barrington has another house here in Genoa. He might have gone there." He drove down the back streets that led to the base of the bluff where he slowed and stared toward a huge, old house tucked into the trees. "Nope. He's not there," Ben said, and sped back to the highway.

He eased his truck cautiously across the railroad tracks in front of the power plant and turned down the narrow road to the left. It paralleled the highway for about a quarter-mile past the huge mountains of coal and then veered sharply to the right toward the river. Before the parking lot was in view, Ben pulled off to the side. "We'll walk from here."

Shrouded in darkness, the moon playing peek-a-boo among the clouds, they could have easily approached the large parking lot undetected from the distant boat ramp, but Ben was taking no chances. He chose to stay close to the tree line in the darkest shadows. Two lights on high poles near the ramp cast an orange glow on that side of the lot, but neither those lights, nor the bright lights from the power plant illuminated the roadway where Ben and Erik made their stealth approach. A half-dozen cars and empty boat trailers rested in the center of the lot, lonely and still with not the slightest sign of human movement anywhere. The white Suburban wasn't there. Ben turned quickly and started trotting back to his truck. "C'mon," he called to Erik. "There's another landing not too far from here."

He wheeled the pickup around and raced back to the highway, heading south on the River Road. "The next one is just a couple of miles… just past the fish hatchery."

To Erik, the one-lane gravel road that Ben turned onto looked as if it went nowhere, even though the sign said "Boat Landing." Several hundred yards from the highway the headlight beams found the embankment of a railroad grade, and the road made a ninety-degree right turn. A ways farther it made a wide left turn and entered into a narrow tunnel-like passage under the tracks.

Ben killed the lights and parked the truck tight against the railroad grade. "We'd better walk from here," he said to Erik.

The darkness seemed more intense at this landing as trees shadowed the narrow roadway. Up ahead they could hear voices, and as they made their way toward the landing, there was no mistaking the white Suburban parked in the small open lot where the moonlight revealed its distinct shape. It appeared as though the pontoon was in the water, and another dark-colored van was backed near the ramp. A flood of light from the rear of the van illuminated the area between it and the pontoon.

Erik and Ben worked their way closer. Plenty of trees created adequate shadows to conceal their approach, and two toilet structures standing off to the side provided the perfect cover.

From there they could see the van was not hooked to a boat trailer, but two men slid a four-foot-long wooden crate out its rear doors that were swung open wide. The crate appeared to be quite heavy. The men struggled and grunted as they carried it to the pontoon. Two more men on the boat leaned down to take hold and hoisted the crate on board. They maneuvered it to the center of the deck while the others returned to the rear of the van and slid out a second crate, identical to the first.

Erik recognized two of the men as being the same ones he saw with Barrington at the truck stop restaurant, but Barrington was nowhere in sight. A stranger stood at the controls of the boat.

"When will you be back with more?" one of the men asked when the second crate was securely on board the pontoon.

"I think there will be four more ready by Monday afternoon, so I'll be here a little after midnight with four more crates."

When four crates had been unloaded from the van and put onto the boat, one of the men closed the van doors, got into the driver's seat and drove off. As the vehicle passed Ben's vantage point he saw the Illinois license plate. By that time, the pontoon's motor was running and it was backing away from the landing with all the other men aboard. Within a few seconds they were out of sight heading downriver.

Erik and Ben sat still in the shadows for a short while listening for any other activity. They only heard the whining of tires on pavement coming from the highway. They stepped out into the parking lot. "Wonder what's in those crates," Erik said.

"We should've brought the boat," Ben mumbled. "We could've followed them."

"You have a boat?"

"Yeah, nothing fancy," Ben replied. "Just a sixteen-foot flat bottom with a forty horse *Mercury*. Good for fishin' in the backwaters."

"That guy driving the van said he'd be back Monday night."

Ben tugged on Erik's arm, urging him to head back to the pickup at the railroad tracks. "Maybe we'll be back here, too... with the boat."

Saturday August 4

All day Saturday seemed to be one of those lazy days when any accomplishment had taken leave, and all ambition was away on vacation. Erik knew that Bert wouldn't call him – he never did on a day after Erik had worked late the night before, and especially on a Saturday. It was almost four o'clock when he and Ben had returned home from their little spy mission, so sleeping in seemed justified.

A quiet knock on the front door didn't arouse Ben stretched out on the living room sofa. He was usually a light sleeper, but the chain of events over the last few days had finally caught up with him. When he had gotten up earlier to use the bathroom, he realized his exhaustion and rather than getting dressed and facing the day, he plopped onto the couch and succumbed to the much needed sleep.

Never needing or expecting an invitation to come in, Troy opened the door and walked in just as he usually did. The knock, he thought, was just a formality – a courtesy to at least announce his arrival. When he found Ben snoring on the couch in only his underwear, the thought crossed his mind to leave and return later, but then he abruptly decided to stay. Erik must be there, as the limo was parked in the driveway. He checked the kitchen and found no one. At the end of the short hallway to the bathroom at the bottom of the stairs he called softly, "Erik?"

"He's probably upstairs sleeping," a drowsy voice came from the living room.

Troy spun on his heels, just a little startled by the answer. "I thought you were asleep," he said to Ben.

"I was. I didn't hear you come in." Ben rose up on one elbow and rubbed his eyes. "What time is it?"

"Little after eleven," Troy replied. "Rough night?"

Ben sat up, stretched and yawned. He blinked a few times to adjust to the sudden deliverance from sound slumber into broad daylight and contemplated the inquiry a few moments. "That depends on what you call rough."

Considering Ben's current state of affairs, Troy knew better than to suggest the possibility of there having been a party, to which he had not been invited. The house was too tidy – the only thing out of place was an empty popcorn bowl.

Before Troy could come up with a clever reply, Ben started to explain the prior night's activities. "Erik and I followed Barrington's Suburban down to the river about midnight. Erik saw him leave town with the pontoon. But it wasn't Barrington."

"And you didn't come get me?" Troy whined.

"They already had a half-hour head start on us, and there just wasn't enough time to come looking for you. Sorry."

Troy was a little disappointed that he had missed out on the excursion, but he understood the circumstances. "So what happened?"

"We finally caught up to them at the boat landing by the fish hatchery."

"What the hell were they doing there at that time of night?"

"Well, you know how dark it is back there at night…"

Troy nodded.

"We left my truck out by the tracks and walked the rest of the way in. Managed to sneak in behind the toilets without them even noticing. There was another van with Illinois license plates, and they were loading some crates from the van onto the pontoon."

"Was it Barrington's drivers?"

"Yeah, a couple for sure. I couldn't get a good look at all of them, but there were about six of 'em." Ben rose from the sofa, padded lazily into the kitchen, and retrieved a can of coffee and filters from the cupboard. Troy followed him and immediately emptied the old grounds and filter from the coffeemaker into the garbage.

"So, what were the crates?" Troy asked.

Ben ran a pitcher of cold water while Troy scooped the coffee into the new filter. "Don't know. They were just plain wooden crates, about four feet long… and they must have been heavy the way those guys were grunting."

Troy slid the filter basket into place and Ben poured the water into the top of the machine. "So, what'd they do with 'em then?"

"One guy got into the van and drove off, and the rest of them left on the pontoon."

"So, what d'ya suppose was in the crates?"

"Well, whatever it was, the guy in the van is coming back with four more Monday night. We overheard that much."

Erik, clad only in shorts, shirtless and barefoot, sauntered into the kitchen, pulled a chair out from the table and sat down. "Overheard what?" he said, trying to catch up to the conversation.

"That the guy in the Illinois van is coming back with more crates Monday night," Ben repeated.

"You still planning on being there to watch?" Erik asked.

"Yeah… with the boat, hiding back in the lagoon."

"So, where d'ya suppose they're taking those crates?" Troy asked.

"That's what I intend to find out," Ben said. "But my guess is an island. You guys heard them mention an island the other night." He went to a cupboard, pulled out three coffee cups and set them on the table.

Troy was already there with the freshly brewed pot of coffee, waiting to pour. "You're gonna let me go along this time, aren't you?"

"I was kinda counting on both of you," Ben said.

Erik took a sip of the hot coffee. "We'll have to get there early, but how do you plan to hide your truck? They'll know your truck, won't they?"

"We'll put the boat in at the power plant landing," Ben said. "It's just a couple of miles. Anyway, we've got all weekend to figure out the details." He collected his cup and headed up the stairway to find some clothes. When he returned a few minutes later, he found the other two hadn't moved. "Feel like grilling some burgers?" he suggested.

The trio spent the afternoon together in the back yard of the little country home grilling, eating, sipping a few beers, tossing around a football, and in general, enjoying each other's companionship. Somehow, the day had managed to ease the tension; Erik finally accepted his gut feelings that maybe he had found his spot in the universe where he belonged. For the first time since he graduated from high school back in Maine, he felt secure among his newfound friends. A job – even though it was just part-time – was keeping him flush for the time being. He would make the final payment to Bert for the new tires with his next paycheck, and although a guilty little lump caught in his throat every now and then, he quickly dismissed the idea of sending back the money his dad had given him by mistake. That was his ticket home, or an emergency cushion, should the need ever arise.

Ben seemed more relaxed, too, than he had in weeks. Perhaps he had accepted the fact that he might not ever see his father again, and now Erik and Troy were providing him with a sense of well being, supporting him in his search for the truth, whatever that might be.

Late that afternoon Ben headed to the garage and lifted the overhead door on the right. Erik had always parked the Mustang in front of that door, but he had never seen it open. That part of the garage had been added to the original; a solid wall separated the two halves, and so Erik had not known what the closed half contained, and he never asked. But now it was no longer a secret: there was Ben's boat on a trailer – a sixteen-foot flat bottom johnboat with a windscreen, steering and controls midship, and a shiny black forty horsepower *Mercury* outboard motor hanging on the transom.

Ben connected the cables from a charger to the battery aboard the boat, just to make certain it was fully charged. He checked the two gas tanks; one was full and the other half. "Remind me to fill this tank before we get to the river," he told Erik who was following his every move about the boat.

"When do you think we should leave?" Erik asked.

"If we go sometime late afternoon, and make it look like just a fishing trip, even if Barrington or those other guys spot us, they won't think anything of it."

"We could even go a different way out of town," Troy added. "Head toward La Crosse first. It would be a little farther, but we'll have plenty of time."

"Good idea," Ben replied. "Hey, Troy. Does your grandpa

still have those high-powered binoculars?"

"Yeah, I'm sure he does."

"S'pose you can borrow them?"

"Sure. We can go see him tomorrow."

The barbeque grill went into action again that evening. Troy and Erik trekked off to the *IGA* store for some steaks while Ben got everything ready.

"Y' know," Erik said. "If I were in Maine tonight, I'd be sitting down to beans and hot dogs."

"How's that?" Troy asked.

"It's kind of a traditional Saturday night dinner in Maine."

"Well," Ben exclaimed. "'Bout the only traditional meal we have here is a Friday night fish fry."

"D' you mean a fish boil?"

"No. Here we generally deep-fry fish... or bake it."

"If you want a fish boil," Troy added, "we'll take you up to Door County sometime. They have fish boils there."

"Where's Door County?" Erik asked.

"'Bout two hundred miles from here... over by Green Bay."

"Green Bay," Erik mumbled. "As in the *Green Bay Packers?*"

"Yep. You don't have a team in Maine, do you?"

"No... we're all Boston fans. Ya know? The Celtics, the Patriots, the Red Sox..."

"The Red Sox," Ben jeered. "When did they last win the Series?"

"Haven't," Erik replied with a sheepish grin. "Not since Babe Ruth."

"Kinda like the Chicago Cubs. They haven't won it since the 1930s. But some of us here in Wisconsin cheer 'em on."

After the satisfying steak dinner, they decided that it would be safe to go to the Central Express coffee shop for a while. They picked a table in the corner.

The place was quite busy for a Saturday night, and there were even a few of the local truck drivers gathered at the big center table. The big man with the gray hair, blue suspenders and dominating voice led the discussion going on there, but the topic somewhat differed from the usual tall tales of life on the road. Ben, Erik and Troy couldn't help but be drawn in like sinners at an Evangelist's tent, listening to a couple of the men who were delivering their views in a style that sounded a bit like an address to Congress.

"I assure you," the big man proclaimed, "because man is a fighting creature, there will always be wars. With the birth rate of the world as it is, and with people living longer, in a couple hundred years, there won't be enough room left on the planet to produce enough food to feed them all.   War is nature's way of readjusting the population."

"Well, that's true," another man broke in. "But we haven't healed the black eye from the last one, yet.   If Dessert Storm proved anything, it proved that all nations are too economically dependent on each another.   And it seems like we rebuild every country we destroy in war, so there's little difference between the spoils of victory and the ruins of defeat."

"Every country," the big man went on, "has always recognized war only as a disagreeable necessity.   Everyone talks about world peace.   But the psychology of a whole nation is such that you can't deal with it like you would a single individual.   Nations are like passionate crowds; a little bit of flag waving and one whiff of national temper will blow years of peace-making sky high."

"Well, let's hope that all the potential war-makers have the moral strength to resist using weapons that assure world supremacy, if they had one within their reach."

"Supremacy gained that way would not last," the big man argued.   "Advantages are always neutralized.   Defense keeps in pace just behind defiance; once the results of the initial surprise have worn off, things have a way of leveling out."

"But consider the consequences.   Modern civilization is always right on the edge.   It teetered in '91, and we're still wobbling from its affects a decade later.   Another shock like that in this unstable condition?   What would happen? Utter collapse? The loss of our freedom?   It could mean misery too horrible to imagine."

"But a situation we must contemplate if we're going to prevent it."

The conversation continued among the men at the center table with a volley of pros and cons of political and military conflict between nations. Erik was convinced that at least one in the group seemed to think that war was essential for the survival of mankind. Ben understood the economic theory – that wartime put a lot of people to work producing military equipment and supplies – he'd studied that topic at college. He grasped, too, the concept of world population problems, but he much preferred alternative solutions instead of the gruesome effects of war.

Sunday August 5

Ben had already completed his early hour workout by the time Troy woke up Sunday morning. Without getting dressed, he ambled down the stairs and into the shower. A few minutes later he poured himself a cup of fresh coffee, and with only a bath towel wrapped around his waist he joined Ben out on the deck. It was just one of the reasons he liked to stay at Ben's place – no neighbors peeping across the back yard, allowing such freedoms that were impossible to enjoy at his house in town.

The arrival of the dawn had been quite spectacular with the sun rising into a brilliant purple sky, and now the edges of the approaching clouds were colored with shades of pink and orange. A cool breeze whispered a hint of summer rain, and as the leading edge of the cloud front gradually erased the remaining clear sky, it was easy to tell that this day wouldn't be ideal for another backyard barbeque.

Ben clasped his hands behind his head and arched his back as Troy sat down in the chair beside him. He contemplated the grayness of the clouds. "Looks like some rain today."

"Yeah, a good day to visit Grandpa," Troy said. "I'll call him later to make sure it's okay for us to come over." He set his coffee cup down. Never wanting to pry into Ben's privacy without an invitation, he thought this situation was getting more serious, and he sincerely wanted to help his best friend. A carefully asked question might get Ben talking. "Anything new about your dad?"

"Troy, I've looked all over hell and half of Georgia... all the places I thought he could be staying, and so far, I haven't found a trace."

"How about relatives? Have you called all of them?"

"Everyone I can think of. None of them have heard from him either."

"I don't get it," Troy mumbled. "How could he just vanish like that?"

"I don't get it either, Troy. I'm running out of ideas."

"Well, maybe when we find out what King and his buddies are up to down at the river..." Troy's voice trailed off. He wasn't sure what that would prove, or how it would help them solve the mystery of Stan Hudson's disappearance. But it might expose Peter Barrington for what he was, and that could lead to some answers.

It was after 11 o'clock when Troy, Ben, and Erik bailed out of the Buick Regal in Grandpa Ernest's driveway. His house was an old, modest, two-story affair with old-fashioned white siding and forest green shutters on all the windows. When Alice was still alive, flowers bloomed everywhere, making it a showplace of color, but as of late, the only blossoms were the sunflowers scattered among the rows of sweet corn in the backyard vegetable garden. Ernest puttered in that garden all summer, every summer. Only the occasional rain showers were keeping him indoors today.

Troy bounded up the porch steps, gave his usual one knock on the screen door, and let himself in. "Hi, Grandpa. We're here."

A delicious fried chicken aroma wafted out into the damp air, luring Ben in, and Erik right behind him. "Hi, Grandpa Ernest," Ben greeted as the old man stepped out of the kitchen to welcome his guests. Ben had always been considered "almost family" in this house, so he felt right at home. He grabbed Erik's elbow and pulled him into the middle of the room. "Grandpa Ernest... this is our friend, Erik."

The elderly gentleman stepped forward, first offering a genuine family-style hug to Ben, as if Ben were one of his own.

"Good to see you again, Ben." Then he turned to Erik and offered a handshake. "Glad to meet you, Erik. How long you been hangin' around with these two hoodlums?" His brow was wrinkled up in a frown, but his voice suggested laughter.

Erik chuckled. "Oh, a couple of months now, I guess." For a long moment he studied the white-haired man's tanned face that showed a good share of life experience in its lines and wrinkles, but he immediately detected the friendly warmth pouring out of those old eyes, and now there was no question from whom Troy had inherited his good nature.

Grandpa Ernest locked his elbow around Ben's neck. "Well, you'd better watch out for this guy... he's a champion fighter, you know." He jostled Ben a little, and Ben just smiled and giggled and offered no resistance. "Of course, he's never beat me in a wrestling match," the old man added.

Erik, momentarily stunned by the statement, stared into Ben's eyes.

"You're absolutely right about that," Ben laughed. Then, to Erik he added, "What Grandpa Ernest really means is that we've *never had* a wrestling match."

The old man released his hold on Ben. "Now, what'd you go tell him that for?" He laughed some more, and then turned back toward the kitchen. "You boys grab a cold beer from the icebox and go sit on the porch. Dinner's not quite ready yet."

Troy, already at the open refrigerator, pulled out three cans and handed one to each of the others as he led them out onto the wide enclosed porch. "Need any help with anything?" he asked his grandfather.

"Naw, you guys just relax. I'll handle the chow."

The padded wicker chairs were a lot more comfortable than Erik thought they looked. Even though the weather was rather dreary and wet, the day was turning out to be quite good, after all. The smell of a good, home cooked Sunday dinner and spending the time among best friends had Erik spinning in a joyous bliss. Or, maybe, he thought, the reason his head was spinning was the beer. He knew he wasn't an experienced drinker – this one he felt, and another would make him stupid.

A half-hour and two brief rain showers had passed when Grandpa Ernest announced from the doorway that the dinner was ready. The boys all sprang from their chairs, their hunger amplified by the tantalizing aromas floating out onto the porch. They followed him into the large kitchen where a table was set for four, and a huge platter of fried chicken at its center.

"Wow!" Erik remarked when he saw all the food. "Fried chicken and all the with-its!"

Ben and Troy looked at him with question marks dripping from their faces. "All the what?" they said in unison.

"With-its," Erik replied matter-of-factly. "You know... potatoes, vegetables, bread... all the with-its."

Ben chuckled. "Oh, Grandpa Ernest. We didn't mention that Erik is from Maine. Sometimes he talks kinda funny."

The old man smiled and winked at Erik. "Well, I didn't think it was funny talk at all. I knew exactly what he meant."

He directed Erik and Ben to opposite sides of the table, and he and Troy sat down at opposite ends. When they were all settled, Grandpa Ernest bowed his head with closed eyes. Ben and Troy expected it, but it caught Erik a little by surprise.

"Heavenly Father," the old gentleman began, "We thank you for this wonderful food. I, in particular, thank you for the rain today, to keep my garden growing, and my table full of *with-its*. And please guide us all in the right directions down life's difficult paths. In your name we pray. Amen."

They all raised their heads, and Ben noticed the quirky little grin on Erik's lips.

"That was a very nice prayer, Sir," Erik said.

"Thank you. And don't call me Sir. You call me Grandpa Ernest like the rest of the younguns." He stabbed into a big piece of chicken with his fork and plopped it on his plate, motioning to Erik and Ben to dig in. He didn't have to make any gestures to Troy, as he already had the large bowl of mashed potatoes hoisted in front of his plate.

"By the way, Grandpa," Troy said. "Can we borrow your binoculars for a few days?"

"Binoculars? I don't have any binoculars."

"Sure you do. Those high-powered ones. They're hanging out in the garage."

Ernest's expression drooped a bit as he was reminded, once again, that his memory wasn't quite what it use to be. "Oh, yeah. I guess I had forgotten about them."

"Well?" Troy repeated. "Is it alright if we use them for a few days? We're going down to the river."

"Sure. Why not?"

By this time, Troy was digging into the huge mound of mashed potatoes on his plate that he had drenched with gravy. He had always been quite fond of mashed potatoes and gravy, and usually finished off a helping of that before starting with the rest. He took a big bite, and almost immediately spit it out onto his plate again, displaying a grimace that was so unlike him, especially at mealtime. "Grandpa! This chicken gravy tastes like wallpaper paste!"

While Ben and Erik looked on in near astonishment, Grandpa Ernest eyed Troy and the gravy bowl with great curiosity. "Uh oh. How long do ya think wallpaper would stay up if it were hung with chicken gravy?"

Troy rinsed out his mouth with a gulp of water. "Maybe a day," he answered in disgust. "Grandpa! You didn't!"

"No, of course not. But I guess we'd better use this stuff to hang the new wallpaper in the den, and maybe you could get that other bowl with the gravy in it from the counter by the sink."

After Troy had scraped his paste-laden potatoes into the garbage and rinsed off his plate, he replaced the misidentified bowl on the table with the very similar gravy bowl, and by then, even he was laughing right along with Ben and Erik – and Grandpa Ernest – about his unfortunate but humorous encounter. Although occasional giggles continued, they all enjoyed the fine dinner.

When the dishes were all washed and put away, the boys retreated to the porch again, and Troy headed out to the garage with Grandpa Ernest to retrieve the binoculars. The rain had let up, so Grandpa headed for his garden. Troy returned to find Ben deeply submerged in thought about something, and he recalled their early morning conversation.   "Penny for your thoughts," said Troy.

Ben gently eased himself out of a subconscious drift and turned to Troy. "Chicken gravy," he replied.

The response drew a smile to Troy's face, but it quickly turned to a puzzled frown when he noticed Ben's austerity. "Chicken gravy? Why are you thinking about chicken gravy?"

Ben leaned forward with elbows on knees and rested his chin on interlaced fingers. "Sometimes things don't appear as they really are... like the chicken gravy and the wallpaper paste."

Troy just stared with wondering eyes, not sure where Ben was going with this conversation.

"What we see King and his guys doing might be something entirely different than what we think it is," Ben explained.

"So, what are they? Wallpaper paste or chicken gravy?"

Monday August 6

Looking every bit the part of fishermen, although they had no intentions of making any serious attempts at landing the big one, Ben, Troy, and Erik were prepared for the wait. After putting the boat into the river at the power plant landing, Ben maneuvered his craft among the islands downriver about two miles through the backwaters near the mouth of the Bad Axe River. He was searching for the perfect vantage point to keep an eye on the Fish Hatchery Boat Landing, and still remain invisible to the men who would soon be at work there. He had explored these backwaters many times on countless fishing trips, so he knew the area. But the river changes; sandbars form and waterlogged driftwood lodge below the surface of the shallow water creating plenty of hazards, even for a shallow draft johnboat with the motor trimmed as high as possible. While there was still a little daylight left, Ben made sure he knew where to point the bow when the time came to move.

They finally decided that just beyond the point of the island opposite the landing offered their best concealment. The boat could be easily hidden, and they could view the landing from the cover of the densely wooded island. Now that they had found their point of surveillance, it was just a matter of waiting.

Making use of a flotation cushion as a pillow, Troy leaned against the side of the boat, stretching across with his feet against the other side. Ben and Erik sat in the two swivel seats by the controls.

"Sure could use a Moxie and a Whoopee Pie right now," Erik announced.

"A what?" Ben asked.

"Moxie. It's kinda like root beer... only stronger. Haven't seen any since I left Maine."

"Must be something local. I never heard of it," Ben replied.

"And I'd bet you're gonna tell us what Whoopee Pie is, too," Troy added.

"You mean you don't have Whoopee Pies here, either?" Erik said a little startled.

"Never heard of that either," Ben said. "What is it?"

"Well, it's two soft chocolate chip cookies – but they're more like cake – with a creamy white filling sandwiched between. They're really good. 'Course, I haven't seen any of them since I left Maine, either."

Ben reached into the cooler at his feet and pulled out an icy can of *Coke*, offering it to Erik. "Here. This is the best I can do for now."

By midnight, even Ben was nodding off. There had been no activity at the landing since darkness closed in completely. It had given Ben about three hours to reflect on the past few months, and to anticipate the future. Thoughts of the past produced a twinge of anger, and the future scared him. He wanted to believe that his father was still alive, but he was finding that belief difficult to support, now, with all the developments that had occurred lately. Barrington was playing rougher than just a hard-hitting businessman; there seemed to be more at stake than a trucking contract, and if Stanley Hudson had interfered with Barrington's plans that were something less than honest, there was little doubt that he would use whatever force necessary to eliminate the interference. His men had already attempted the use of deadly force against Ben, and it was quite likely he – or his thugs – had been more successful in dealing with Stan Hudson. Now, Ben's most serious hope was to learn what had happened, and to perhaps discover some needed evidence that would convince the police that Stan Hudson was not simply hiding from his creditors.

All these thoughts made Ben suddenly conscious of a great longing for the comfort of his father's presence. It bored into him like a honeybee bores into a blossom. He wondered if he'd ever get over missing his dad, and he thought maybe he really didn't want to. But it was an awful feeling sometimes.

Some people said that time would make it easier. But it just wasn't the same – nothing could be the same. Growing up in a small town kept fathers and sons close, somehow, and now the loneliness seemed unavoidable. Even a ringer at horseshoes or a homerun in a softball game just wouldn't be the same without Dad watching and cheering.

It was Troy who aroused Ben and Erik when the headlights of a vehicle coming down the dark road faintly illuminated the trees on the island. After his restful nap, he had quietly left the boat and made his way through the trees to a spot on the island where he had a clear view of the landing, not more than fifty yards away. Obviously, the thick treetop canopy blocked sunlight here, allowing minimal ground vegetation to grow among the trees at the center of the island, but that made for easy navigation on foot. Ben and Erik followed him to the edge of the woods where tall reeds and brush received enough sunlight to flourish, providing a natural blind and a perfect observation point.

From that far away, with only the light of the moon, details were obscured, but the vehicle backing the trailer and pontoon down the boat ramp was unmistakably Barrington's white Suburban. Ben hoisted the binoculars to his eyes and watched as three men put the pontoon into the water. The binoculars seemed to magnify even the smallest amount of light, and he could identify one of the men as Lenny King. The others, he thought, were the foreigners who he had seen several times before.

A short while after the pontoon was afloat and nosed up to the edge of the water, another pair of headlights briefly lit up the ramp area as it turned, and then backed toward the pontoon. Ben recognized the van as the same one they had seen there in the wee hours of Saturday morning. The driver got out, came to the rear of the van and swung the doors open. And just as they had witnessed before, four heavy crates were loaded onto the pontoon boat.

"Let's get back to the boat," Ben whispered. "They're gonna pull out soon, and I want to be ready to follow them."

By the time they were back aboard the johnboat, they could hear the drone of the pontoon's outboard motor heading away from the landing. Ben eased his craft out from behind the island, and once he knew for sure that the Illinois van had left the ramp area, he pulled out into the channel just in time to see the lights of the pontoon disappear around the bend.

"They're heading out to the main channel," Troy suggested.

Ben left the running lights off and followed the pontoon at a safe distance that he knew would not be noticed, while Erik kept a close watch with the binoculars. They had gone several miles downriver when Erik saw the pontoon turn toward what he thought was the western shore of the river.

"No," Ben corrected him. "That's a bunch of islands. We're still a long ways from Iowa." He slowed the motor to just more than an idle as he noticed that they were gaining on the pontoon. He didn't want to get too close.

Among the maze of islands, only the ripples from the wake of the pontoon disturbed the water's surface in the still, night air. Erik's vigilant watch kept the craft in sight until it maneuvered around a point of land and then just seemed to vanish. When Ben saw the lights disappear, he stopped the johnboat motor, as he thought Barrington had beached the pontoon and turned off the lights.

"They just vanished," Erik said.

Troy already had a paddle over the side, pushing the boat silently toward the point where they had last seen the pontoon. Ben grabbed another paddle and joined in the effort. When they reached the point, there was nothing – no beached pontoon or its passengers or cargo.

"Where'd they go?" Erik said.

"They must've gotten around the end of the island," Ben offered. "But the question is: How?" It seemed curious that the pontoon could have slipped away; their only route from that point would have been within the boys' range of sight.

The hum of the huge engines of a barge towboat coming up-river masked all other sounds. Not only did they lose sight of the pontoon, but now they had lost any detection by audible means, too.

Ben started the motor and idled the flat bottom among the islands in hopes of spotting the pontoon beached somewhere, or possibly catch sight of it again on the move. After about a half-hour of an unsuccessful search, Ben suddenly killed the motor.

"What are you doing?" Erik asked.

"Shhhhhh. I thought I heard an outboard," Ben whispered. He cocked his head to one side, listening.

Troy and Erik listened carefully, too, and they both nodded in agreement that the distant sound was the same drone they had heard from Barrington's pontoon motor when it left the landing. Ben started his motor again and aimed the johnboat toward the sound, back in the direction where they had lost track of their prey. When they passed by the point, wavelets were splashing on the shoreline, meaning the pontoon was not far ahead. As they rounded the last island, the pontoon's running lights appeared upriver in the main channel.

"Well, they're heading back to the landing," Ben said. "Not much more we can do now."

Tuesday August 7

It was about five o'clock Tuesday afternoon when Erik returned to the house after working most of the day. With only a couple of hours sleep, he was beat, almost too tired to eat. He plopped down on the living room couch.

Troy knocked once and bounded into the kitchen where Ben was just starting to prepare a meal. "What's for supper?" he asked jokingly.

"Mac and cheese and hot dogs," Ben replied.

"Sounds good. Got enough for one more?"

"Sure. But it'll cost ya."

"I've been thinking, Ben. That spot where we lost Barrington's pontoon last night – think you can find it again?"

"Sure. I know right where it is."

"Well, maybe we should check it out in the daylight."

"Yeah, I've thought about that, too."

"Check out what?" Erik asked, rubbing his eyes as he walked into the middle of the conversation.

"The island where we lost the pontoon... in the daylight."

"I thought about that all day," Erik said.

Three minds all thinking independently alike meant that the idea was worth pursuing.

"Ya know," Ben said, "you guys don't have to go if you don't want to."

"Bert wants me to work tomorrow night, so I know I'll have Thursday free," Erik offered.

"And I don't have anything better to do, either," Troy added.

"Besides," Erik said. "It might be dangerous for you to go alone."

Danger had been a common element in day-to-day activity lately, so companionship – maybe for safety's sake – wouldn't be such a bad idea. Ben readily accepted the offers. "Okay. Let's plan on Thursday morning. We'll make a day of it, and maybe we could even camp for a few nights on a sandbar."

Ben had everything ready for the outing by Wednesday night – tent, sleeping bags, a cooler packed with food, and all the other miscellaneous camping gear was loaded in the boat. There was always plenty of firewood available on the islands – driftwood from the spring floods and dead, fallen trees – but Ben packed a big bag of charcoal and the grille in the boat, just in case. He figured he had enough food to last the three of them a couple of days, at least, and they wouldn't be too far from DeSoto or Lansing if they needed something.

When Erik arrived home that night a little past eleven o'clock,

Troy was already at the house. Ben had picked him up earlier, and he planned to stay the night there, ready for an early morning departure to the river. He, too, had a cooler full of food and refreshments, a bedroll, and a duffel bag with a few extra clothes.

"When do you have to be back to work?" Ben asked Erik.

"I told Bert I'd be gone on a camping trip for a few days. He doesn't expect me back 'til next week."

"Great. This'll be just great. Four days out on the river. I haven't done this for a while."

"Last summer," Troy reminded him.

By the tone of Ben's voice and his perky behavior, Erik knew that this trip would be good therapy for him. Perhaps it would give him a chance to relax a little and let him think about something else besides his missing father for a while. On the other hand, whatever they might find on one of those Mississippi islands might make the situation tenser, so Erik knew he had to be ready for that, too.

Thursday August 9

Thursday morning flooded into Erik's room with brilliant sunshine, such that he just couldn't stay in bed longer than thirty seconds after he opened his eyes. The day was already trying to lure him out. He glanced at his alarm clock that he had set for eight. It was only seven-thirty, and he was wide-awake. Then he remembered the plans for the day – plans that would begin a long weekend with his best friends out on the river. He hadn't taken any extra time off from his job since he started there in June, and it would be good to get away for a few days. This would be a new experience for him, too, spending some time on the Mississippi River. It probably wouldn't be that much different from the camping trips he and his friends went on back in Maine, along the streams and lakes, out in the north woods wilderness. He was ready for a new adventure, just the same.

His backpack that he had traveled with from Maine was the only thing he had to carry some clothes and personal needs. He pulled it from the closet and stuffed in a pair of blue jeans, a couple of T-shirts, some socks and underwear, and his favorite pair of shorts. He'd wear his second favorite pair today.

At the top of the stairs as he headed down to the bathroom for a shower, he peeked in the open door to Ben's room. Troy was still asleep in the big king-sized bed, but Ben was evidently already up and stirring. "Hey, Troy," Erik called out. "Sun's shinin'… you gonna sleep all day?"

Troy let out a mournful groan that resembled something like the sound of a chainsaw running out of gas. "Yeah, I'm awake. Just working up the ambition to get up." He threw back the covers and swung his feet out onto the floor.

Erik trotted down the stairs to the shower. When he was drying off, Troy stumbled in, still half-asleep, dropped his shorts on the floor and went into the shower stall. "Hope you left some hot water for me," he mumbled. "This'll be the last shower we get for a few days, ya know."

"Yeah, I know," Erik responded. "We go camping in Maine, too."

Ben already had the boat trailer hooked up to the truck and was checking the turn signals on the trailer when Troy and Erik came out the front door with duffel bag and backpack. He'd been up since sunrise, so he had a good head start on the other two. "I'm pretty sure we have everything. I've checked it all over a couple of times. Do you know of anything we're missing?" He was directing his question to Troy, because Troy had been on these river camping trips before. Erik wasn't sure if it was the anticipation of the four days of camping, or the expectations of a spy mission that excited Ben, but whatever it was, it had Ben in high spirits. That was a good thing. He hadn't seen Ben this enthusiastic… ever.

Troy took a survey of all the gear in the boat. "I see a hatchet, but I don't see a regular axe. You got one in here?" Troy quizzed. "And how about the saw? Let's take the saw, too, if we find some big wood."

"Good idea," Ben said. He sauntered into the open garage and emerged with the extra tools. "Anything else?"

"Not that I can think of now," Troy said.

Erik tossed his backpack into the bow of the boat right next to Troy's duffel. In his mind's eye he silently took inventory of the things he'd packed, naming off the pieces of clothing, toothbrush, toothpaste, soap, towels, camera, flashlight, pocket knife, wallet... yup... he was ready to go.

With everything secure at the house and the Mustang locked in the garage, the threesome climbed into the cab of Ben's truck. Considering the seriousness of the original purpose for going to the river that day, the thought of a mini-vacation had put them all in lighter spirits.

"Hi, ho, Silver," Ben joked as he aimed the truck and trailer out the driveway.

About five miles down the highway Troy asked, "Where ya plannin' to put the boat in?"

"Think maybe we'll go down by the bridge at Lansing."

"Why so far down?"

"We'll be closer to the better camping islands and not so far away from the marina if we need gas."

"But I thought you would want to camp somewhere close to where King is going... so we can keep an eye on it."

"We will. That place isn't too far above Lansing, ya know."

That was good enough for Troy. Ben knew that stretch of the river quite well. Even in total darkness the other night, he had recognized where they were.

"And besides," Ben added. "I think we'll take Erik up to the lookout by Genoa on the way down, so he can get a better understanding of what the river is like."

"What about Mt. Hosmer – the park above Lansing, too?" Troy suggested.

"Sure. We'll go up there, too."

Erik read the signboard on Highway 35 that said: SCENIC OVERLOOK. When Ben finally reached the top of the winding, steep hill road and nosed the truck up to the rock retaining wall at the edge of the parking lot, Erik got his first *real* glimpse of the grandeur of the Mississippi River Valley. From there, the panoramic view of miles up and down the river, and the Minnesota bluffs on the other side seemed rather staggering to Erik. "I never imagined it was *this* big," he said, his voice drenched in awe.

They all got out of the truck and stood by the rock wall where they were some six hundred feet above the river surface. "This is the main channel right below us," Ben explained, "And if you follow the line of buoys there, you can see where the channel crosses over, around those islands to the Minnesota side." Then he pointed Erik's attention downriver. "That's the Genoa lock and dam, and that big building with the tall smokestack just beyond it is the power plant. Remember? That's where we checked the one boat landing the other night."

Erik nodded and just continued to gaze at the magnificent vista before him. After a couple of minutes it dawned on him to get out his camera. He needed some pictures of this view. He thought maybe this was more spectacular than some of the sights from the mountaintops in Maine.

"C'mon," Ben urged. "Let's head on down to Lansing. You'll get a better look at some of the big islands from the overlook down there." He had to practically drag Erik back to the truck. Erik didn't want to leave this fantastic view.

But at the Lansing City Park high on Mt. Hosmer above the town and overlooking the river, Erik got another eyeful. This was equally as breathtaking as the last overlook, and from here, looking down on the landmasses surrounded by water, he could understand the vast area of some of the islands, as Ben had described to him. He shot some more pictures.

"That's the marina right below us," Ben said, and then he pointed upriver toward the horizon. "And you can just barely see the smokestack at the Genoa power plant. Do ya see it?"

Erik searched a bit. "Yeah, I see it. How far is that?"

"About thirteen miles," Ben replied.

"And where's the island we're going to?"

Ben pointed vaguely. "It's about four or five miles from here... in those backwaters. You can't really see the main channel up there because of the trees."

Ben pulled into the *Kwik Star* on Main Street so they could get some donuts and coffee to go, and then they headed back across the river to the boat landing about a mile from the Blackhawk

Bridge. It was about eleven o'clock when Ben backed the boat down the ramp and into the water. Twenty minutes later, they emerged into the main channel, heading upriver, and in another twenty they were slowly cruising among the backwater islands where they had been just a few nights ago.

It all looked so much different, now, in broad daylight. The heavily wooded islands all looked the same to Erik, but he felt confident that Ben seemed familiar with the surroundings.

"Right here is where we lost the pontoon," Ben said. He scanned the shoreline of the island and looked beyond the far end where the verdant foliage seemed to blend into the next island behind it. "Let's find a campsite for now. We can come back here later and take a closer look around."

"Good idea," Troy said. "I'm getting hungry."

"Me too," Ben replied. "How 'bout you, Erik? You ready for some chow?"

"Is the Pope Catholic?"

Ben turned the boat toward another island that he remembered as a good potential camping spot. It was close to the route King had taken, but obscure enough for a campsite to remain hidden from view.

"How does this look?" Ben asked as he idled the johnboat toward a stretch of sandy beach strewn with a good supply of dry-looking driftwood and dead, fallen trees. Beyond the beach was a stand of tall, green timber on high and dry ground. There were no signs of other people in any direction, and this seemed the perfect place to spend a few days. To Erik, it looked like a paradise, and he was eager to set foot on this land, as if he were the first explorer to ever walk upon its beach.

"Wonder why no one else has found this place," Troy said to no one in particular.

Ben killed the motor and raised the lower unit out of the water. "Water's too shallow to get a boat up to it," he said. They were about fifteen yards short of the sandy beach, and using the paddles the rest of the way eliminated the chance of wrecking the propeller on some unseen hazard.

Barefoot and shirtless they waded in shin-deep water, dragging the flat-bottomed craft up onto the sand as far as it would easily go. Erik ambled along the beach a ways, and then returned to the boat. "This feels like we're the first people to ever walk here," he said, sort of wrapped up in the sense of adventure.

"Well, I hate to rain on your parade," Ben said. "But I've been here before... once when Dad and I were fishing. We didn't camp overnight, though."

Erik gazed around their utopia, not spotting any telltale signs that this had ever been a popular recreational getaway – no charred remnants of prior campfires, no tracks in the sand, no chopped-off branches, or even a single empty beer can or candy wrapper. The place seemed untouched by human hands even though Ben said he'd been there before.

Troy was already scouting the woods for a good campsite. He called out, "Hey Ben... Erik... come here and look at this." Just inside the tree line he had found a small clearing on a knoll. The ground was sandy and level – perfect for a tent. And just when Erik thought they might be the first to settle in here, he stumbled over the rocks of a fire ring hidden by the long grass. Someone *had* camped here before, but it appeared as though it was quite some time ago.

"This is great," Ben exclaimed. "We can hide the boat easy enough, and no one will ever know we're here. Let's get the tent up and cook some food. I'm starved."

"Okay," Troy said. "But I've got a better idea. Let's cook some food and *then* set up the tent."

That seemed to meet everyone's approval. Ben gathered firewood and started a good, crackling fire in the ring while Troy and Erik toted the coolers and three folding lawn chairs from the boat. It didn't take long for a dozen hot dogs to disappear.

Ben's tent was a large nylon dome, rather quick and easy to construct. After a couple more trips from the boat, they had everything they needed to comfortably spend the next four days, with the exception of, perhaps, a trip to the grocery store in Lansing for more food and ice.

"Okay," Ben said when the campsite seemed to be in good order, "Does anyone feel like going for a little boat ride and maybe some exploring?"

Not much coaxing was necessary, for Troy and Erik were on their feet within seconds of Ben's query.

"I guess I can take that as a 'yes'." He dug to the bottom of his duffel bag, pulled out his .22 caliber target pistol, and stuck it under his belt.

"What's that for?" Troy asked with raised eyebrows.

"Ummmm… snakes. You never know when you might run across a mean snake out here."

Ben made several slow passes by the island where they had lost track of King and the pontoon. It just didn't make any sense. There were no coves or inlets where they could have hidden a boat the size of Barrington's pontoon. There was no sand beach here, but instead, what appeared to be rather deep water right up to a high bank where the trees and brush started.

"Are you sure this is the right place?" Troy asked.

"As sure as my name is Benjamin Hudson."

"Can I make a suggestion?" Erik said.

"I'm listening," Ben replied.

"Let's find someplace to tie up the boat and walk the shore line. Maybe there's something we're just not seeing from out here."

"That's not a bad idea," Ben said. "I saw a good place to tie up down on that point." He nodded toward the end of the island and idled the boat to where a small sandbar protruding from the bank would give them easy access to the shore.

Unlike the island where they were camped, this one had thick, brushy growth along its bank. They were at least fifty feet from the edge of the water where the vegetation thinned, and where they could see to walk. A thick overhead canopy kept the ground in deep shadow, and had this been anytime other than daylight hours, this would have been a very, very dark place. Ben led the way through the shadows. Even there, where the sun had no chance of reaching the ground, the air hung hot and humid, typical August weather along the Upper Mississippi. Insects hummed about them, and in the distance some crows squawked.

The underbrush seemed to be crowding the three explorers farther inland, away from the shoreline. After walking quite some distance, Ben stopped abruptly and raised a warning hand. Troy and Erik stepped up beside him. Just a few yards ahead lay the reason the brush was flourishing here.

"A canal," Ben whispered.

"Where does it go?" Troy said. "I don't remember seeing any canal coming off this island."

"Neither did I," Ben replied. He stepped closer and looked both directions up and down the canal. To the left, toward the closest side of the island, the waterway curved out of sight. To the right, it continued on toward the center of the island, wide and deep enough to carry a good-sized craft. Ben motioned for the other two to follow as he started toward the river end of the canal.

Just past the bend, they discovered why they had not seen the mouth of the canal from the river. Suspended by cables from large oaks on either side of the canal was a sort of gate made with reeds and other foliage woven and tied to wire netting to form a huge, natural-looking curtain. It hung down into the water, as if the reeds were growing there, and the whole thing just blended into the brush on either side of the canal. It was split in the middle, so a boat could pass through by simply pushing the curtain aside, and then it would close up again behind the craft, concealing the waterway from view out in the river. There was no wonder, now, why they had lost sight of the pontoon that night.

"Somebody wants to keep this place a secret," Erik said.

"That somebody would be Peter Barrington," Troy said.

"Or the guys working for him," Ben suggested.

"Why d'ya suppose they're going to this much trouble?" Erik wondered out loud.

"Has something to do with those crates," Ben said. "C'mon. Let's follow the canal, but we'd better be quiet and careful in case someone else is on this island."

Not knowing what they might find – or who – they made their stealthy way along the bank of the canal, ready to disappear into the brush if danger should threaten. They had penetrated the island so deeply that Erik was thinking they might soon hear native drums and see thatched huts. All around them brooded a profound silence that was almost disturbing.

Ben knew of other canals running across islands, and some that were merely a dead-end lagoon – no outlet on the opposite side of the island. But he couldn't recall ever encountering this one before.

"There's something creepy about this place, if you ask me," Troy whispered.

"I think this might be an old Indian burial ground," Ben said. "I think I saw a mound back there a ways."

Up ahead, the canal widened to a large pool where it seemed to dead-end. Ben was the first to notice a couple of small runabouts tied at a simple dock structure on the opposite side. He motioned for his companions to duck out of sight as he, too, crouched down in the brush.

Gruff voices barked out of the trees on the far side of the waterway, and they certainly didn't sound friendly. A sharp pang of distress shot through Ben as two men appeared, both toting rifles. Ben, Troy, or Erik had not seen them before, unless they were of the group that had helped load the crates on the pontoon. Their dark, leathery faces with a couple of days' growth of black beard grimaced and growled, scanning the immediate area around them, as if they knew someone was intruding on their privacy. Ben was glad they were on the other side of the canal where they at least had some chance of staying out of sight – by the looks of those two, they might kill for whatever it was they were guarding. He hoped the brush and weeds veiled their presence well enough to remain undetected by the two hostile men.

Lying as still and as flat as a living room rug they watched and waited until the gunmen appeared satisfied that they had heard animals or birds. They seemed to relax from their watchful tension as the rifles dropped to their sides and they once again disappeared to an obscure hiding place in the woods.

Certain that they were no longer within the gunmen's sight, Ben motioned to Troy and Erik to quietly make a retreat to the johnboat waiting at the far point of the island. This was no place to be lounging the time away. Not speaking a word between them, they made their way through the woods to the boat, climbed aboard, and headed back to their camp.

"What d'ya s'pose that's all about?" Troy said when he finally started breathing normally again.

"Well, they're hiding something on that island," Ben said.

"D'ya think it could be a drug smuggling operation?" Erik added.

"Could be," Ben said. "But drug smugglers usually have faster boats."

Troy and Erik chuckled at the thought. But their faces still displayed concern; some pretty rough-looking characters with guns had confronted them, and even Ben didn't quite know how to proceed from here.

"Maybe we should just go to the cops," Erik suggested.

Ben threw him a worried glance. "Wouldn't do any good," he said. "I've tried to get them to check other things out, and now they don't even listen anymore."

They pulled the johnboat up onto the beach, hiding it behind a fallen tree, and quickly retreated to their campsite where they felt a certain degree of security, just because it was fairly well concealed. It was already past five o'clock. "What d'ya say we get some supper ready," Troy suggested. This spy stuff is making me hungry."

All that evening, they sat at ease watching the river as the shadows grew longer, and eventually, everything blended together in a deep purple haze as the last of the twilight drained from the world. The constant, steady drone of the barge towboats drifted across the river valley, and at long intervals the rumble of freight trains announced their movement along the riverbanks. Hazy fog settled in over the water giving off an eerie white glow in the moonlight and gently masked the dark horizons. Long ago the squeaks and squawks of the river birds had ceased, and the crackling of the campfire was the only immediate interruption of the serenity surrounding the island.

"Got any ideas about what's goin' on up that canal?" Erik asked Ben. He had noticed Ben's restlessness with the sound of any small watercraft in the distance.

Ben had been giving it a lot of thought, but so far, he hadn't come up with any logical answers. He just pressed his lips tightly together, closed his eyes and shook his head.

It was well past midnight when Ben thought there was little point in waiting and expecting Barrington's pontoon to pass that night. Erik had kept busy feeding the campfire, but he finally gave in to the comfort of his air mattress and sleeping bag in the tent. Troy retrieved two sleeping bags and spread them on the sand at the edge of the beach near the dying fire. There, he and Ben kept vigil over the river channel until sleep finally came to them, too.

Three more days passed while the boys fished in the backwaters among the islands, occasionally went for a swim, and generally enjoyed their time in this little paradise where no one interrupted their privacy. Here, out of touch with the mainland and people, they were out of reach of dangers and conflicts in a clean and simplified world reduced to their campsite, boat, water and sky, and a vast number of unseen fish. Here they could relax and let sunshine and moonlight and a sense of peace wash over them with the breeze.

They kept a rather close eye on the channel leading to the mystery island's camouflaged canal entrance. They saw no one coming or going, but they experienced little desire to further investigate the island's interior, knowing heavily armed guards protected it from curious intruders.

Friday August 17

Ben had left for the evening, and hadn't given much indication as to where he might be going, other than to say he wanted to go fishing alone, as he sometimes did. Erik knew that was his way of clearing his mind. Ben liked spending time by himself, with no one to distract his thoughts with a conversation that he didn't want to have.

And there was no point in hoping that Troy would stop by –

he had mentioned earlier in the day that he and Mandy had planned a night in La Crosse for dinner and a movie, and knowing Mandy, she would convince Troy to visit a bar or two afterwards, which meant that it would be well past the wee hours when they returned. Not that she was some sort of bar fly, she just liked the excitement of getting out and mingling with people, dancing to the music of a live band – a break from what she called the monotony of her dull life in a small town and a dead-end job at the truck stop.

Left to himself, Erik experienced a sense of depression. After the adventures of the last few days, he thought a quiet night at home would tend to be rather boring. But relaxing for a while had put him in a state of tiredness that drained him of any ambition to go out, and he didn't know where he would go if he did. Nothing on TV had interested him, so for a while he sat listening to the radio, but that, too, seemed flat and uninspiring.

A curious sense of being watched came over him, but he knew he was alone, and he thought that he should credit their experiences with the unknown over the past few days to putting his nerves a little on edge. Although it was only nine o'clock, Erik considered that maybe just going to bed would be the best thing to do. But tired as he was, a certain restlessness convinced him that he would never get to sleep, and it occurred to him that a long walk out in the fresh air might either revive his ambition, or induce that state of sudden fatigue and make sleep come easier. Either way, it would be better than sitting there regretting idle time. He decided to stroll to the edge of town, and then determine from there if he wanted to continue any farther.

At the fence line where the driveway turned toward the road, Erik paused for a moment to check his pockets for keys and wallet, and perhaps to reconsider a drive in the car instead of hiking in the dark. Just then, a sharp "pop" cut through the stillness, instantly followed by something zinging past his head, and then cracked as it slammed into the old barn foundation. The moment he heard it, he ducked down, out of pure instinct, to make less of a target, and ran, stooped over, along the lane until he was past the old barn, plunging into the small grove of trees behind it.

It was nearly total darkness by then, but there was just enough light for Erik to avoid the tree trunks as he rapidly and silently made his way to the back of the grove. Upon reaching that point, he dropped to the ground, confident that he must be out of sight from whoever had fired the shot.

"For Chrissake!" he muttered to himself. A host of thoughts raced through his head. There was no doubt that this gunman was probably associated with Barrington... or the men working for him. And there was little doubt that this incident was intended to eliminate the interruption of plans – whatever they were. Erik couldn't help but think of Troy and Ben right at that moment. Had the thugs waited for them to separate, and then ambush each one when they were vulnerable? Were they, too, in mortal danger? Or was this a case of mistaken identity? Did the shooter assume he was aiming at Ben in the dark?

The night was quiet, with just a slight breeze that blew across the hills but made very little sound. Erik stayed put for several minutes, just listening, but he heard nothing other than his own heart drumming in his chest. Moving now did not seem so dangerous, as the gunman wouldn't see him any better than he could see the gunman. Still crouching, he stepped cautiously among the trees to the backside of the old barn and peeked around the corner where he had a clear view of the house, the driveway, and a short length of the uphill road into town. He could see the pale yellow glow from the living room window, and though the roofs of the buildings were outlined against the sky, everything else below them was in deep shadow where all detail was lost. There was no sign of the gunman, but Erik wasn't about to take any unnecessary risks. He waited there under cover of the old barn wall foundation shadow for nearly a quarter of an hour, just in case the intruder was still near, hiding in some equally obscure spot. The silence was all at once broken by another little pop and the ping of a bullet ricochet that died away, off in some opposite direction. Erik smiled. Whatever his enemy was firing at, he could not conceive, but it certainly wasn't at him.

He carefully hoisted himself up onto the sill of a window opening where he could peer over the top of the foundation stones with a better vantage point of the surroundings. He still couldn't see any details, but just then, he heard a car engine start and the gravel crunching under its tires down on the road. The sound seemed to be moving toward town, and then headlights abruptly lit the road in front of a car racing up the hill. Erik couldn't identify the car in the darkness, but a bit of white shone among the red of the right taillight, as if the lens were broken. Erik was confident, now, that the car carried the attacker who had obviously admitted to failure for the time being – *if* his objective had been to kill. He considered following the car, but he realized that by the time he could get to the Mustang by the garage and give chase, that car and its driver could be in the next county.

But he had a good idea of where that car was headed. And as long as he was now quite wide awake, there was no point in going back to the house, or even trying to get any sleep until he knew Ben and Troy were safe. If he knew where to start looking for them, he would. But he didn't have a clue. So the most logical action seemed to be to drive to Genoa and search for a car with a broken taillight. He would begin at the big, spooky mansion on the hillside.

Erik parked the Mustang on Water Street next to the Genoa Inn. If there were a Barney Fife or Andy Taylor in this little town, they would surely not question an unfamiliar car parked next to a motel. And this was less conspicuous than parking on the Main Street near any of the bars where it might be recognized, but only a couple of blocks away and within easy walking distance. The big mansion was only a few blocks farther.

For a small town, there seemed to be a lot of activity so late at night, as Main Street was lined with cars, and it wasn't difficult to blend in with the pedestrians sauntering to and from the places of entertainment. Food and drink seemed to be a big industry in this little burg, and after all, Erik remembered, this was a popular river town for sport fishing, and its nightlife was probably like this all summer long.

Loud country music blared from the establishments as the doors opened and patrons entered and left. Erik noticed that no one paid him any attention, and he thought it would probably be quite easy to cruise through and scan the faces. But he wasn't old enough to enter a bar in Wisconsin, and he wasn't going to try. That could only cause trouble for him that he didn't need right now. So he plodded down the sidewalk so that he was facing the rears of the cars parked on that side, crossed over and came back, studying the taillights of every car. He saw one dirty, old Ford with the right side taillight smashed, but the lens was nearly gone, and Erik knew this wasn't the car he had seen earlier.

It was a simple matter to find the big old house that Erik had seen only once before in daylight. He pictured in his mind the substantial building; the front faced with stone, and spires and dormers, three stories tall. It stood in a hollow against the bluff and was surrounded on all sides except the front with oaks and maples. One of the largest and oldest residences in the town, it was said to have grown to such enormity as the result of an addition constructed with the salvaged remains of a sunken riverboat in the late 1800s. It was a sight to behold with its sloped lawn and well-kept flowerbeds flanking the long, steep driveway. But now, in the murky darkness, the moonlight masked by a blanket of heavy clouds, the structure was mostly in shadow. Only the dim rays from the nearest streetlight on the opposite corner penetrated the distance across the yard to the front portico.

Staying in the darkest shadows, Erik gazed at the four vehicles parked on the level pad directly in front of the house. One of them looked like the maroon Dodge Intrepid that Erik had seen at the truck stop on many occasions – it belonged to Lenny King – and the others appeared to be expensive foreign models – Mercedes and Jaguars, perhaps, – that he could not recall seeing before. The place looked deserted – no visible activity, and no light showing from any windows to the front. But a house that size would surely have chambers in the back or on the sides that were not apparent from his vantage point. He could sneak through the trees to investigate that, but his first order of business was to inspect the cars for a broken taillight lens, and the only one he really suspected was the Dodge.

He crept up the driveway, past the black iron picket fence,

keeping to one side in the darkest shadows. When he neared the cars, he crouched as low as possible and was almost crawling on hands and knees to get to the back of the Intrepid. Just as he expected, rubbing his fingers across it revealed the right taillight lens was cracked with a small piece missing from the center. That didn't exactly prove that it was Lenny King shooting at him earlier, but it was a pretty good indication that this was the get-away car. And if it had been King, what was this bunch of thugs up to that was worth the acts of violence they had displayed? And what were they hiding on that island on the Mississippi? And why was Stanley Hudson missing without a trace?

Erik felt a cold, tingling sensation penetrate his whole body. He realized, now, how close he was placing himself to danger, just by being there, and especially alone. But helping his friend track down the reason for his father's disappearance seemed worth the risk. He thought he would sneak around to the back of the house, and maybe see or hear what was going on inside.

Then a sudden noise in the dark behind him jerked him from his mental wandering. He turned quickly, only to see the dark figure of a man standing before him.

"Why do you look at my car?" the man said in an angry sort of tone.

Erik froze. He thought of trying to catch the man off guard with one of his offensive wrestling moves, but the man stood a little too far away for that to be effective.

"Don't try anything funny," the man said, "Or I kill you where you stand."

Erik couldn't see the man's face in the dark, but he had referred to the car as "his car," so Erik assumed this must be Lenny King. "Why did you shoot at me earlier tonight, Lenny?"

There was a short silence, as if the man was surprised with that remark. "I... I know nothing about what you say." There was another short pause, and then the man spoke again. "Turn around and walk to the front door of the house. I have a gun."

"You won't shoot me here, Lenny."

"And what makes you think that?"

"Cause then you'd have a body to get rid of..."

"Be quiet… and start walking."

Erik turned and complied with the order. Even though this man – Lenny King – spoke clearly, his use of English seemed a little odd. Just the way he put words together gave the impression that Lenny was a foreigner with an American-sounding name.

Another of the men who Erik had seen often at the truck stop met them inside the door. His look of astonishment turned to a sneer. "What is he doing here?"

"I found him snooping around outside," Lenny said.

So much for getting a job with the company, now, Erik thought.

The two men exchanged a short conversation in some foreign language, but Erik suspected they were discussing his fate. Then, from behind, Lenny grabbed Erik's wrists and held his arms away from his sides while the other man patted him down, evidently looking for a weapon. When they were satisfied that Erik was unarmed, the second man started up the stairway to the left. Lenny prodded Erik in the back. "Up the stairs," he said, and gave him an aggressive push toward the steps.

Erik followed up a flight of stairs and along a carpeted corridor, all the time Lenny remaining close at his heels. They climbed yet another flight of stairs, and at the end of a narrow passage, the leader unlocked a door and threw it open. "In there," was all he said.

There was no light in the room, and Erik hesitated. "My dear friend," he protested, "I never did like the dark – "

"No words – get in," Lenny interrupted.

Erik eyed the two men. They were both lean and wiry, looking quite capable of holding their own in a rough-and-tumble, but both were armed, and the odds were absurd. So with all resignation, Erik passed through the doorway.

"There will be someone outside this door all night," came the unpleasant voice of his captor, "so, no tricks."

And then the door was shut on utter darkness and the key turned.

Restlessness had overwhelmed Ben late in the afternoon to the point at which it would have been impossible for him to relax that night. Without any explanation of his actual plans, he said he was going fishing – alone – got in the truck and left with the boat trailer in tow.

Under a dismal, overcast sky, he put the boat in at the power plant landing, and headed downriver. Any other time, the weather would have pre-empted a fishing excursion on the river, especially this late. The hot, muggy air felt and smelled like rain, and the forecast had mentioned the strong chance of a late-night thunderstorm. But he wasn't afraid of a little rain – he'd been caught by rain out on the river many times before. Common sense had always prompted him to take cover on an island or the nearest shore until the heavy weather passed, and that had always provided him ample safety.

This night, he planned to use the stormy weather to his advantage. Mystery Island – as they had come to calling it – and the unseen activities there were heavy on his mind, and although he was fairly satisfied that his father was not there, he was quite convinced that Barrington's men were responsible for his disappearance, and whatever kind of business they were conducting on that island was somehow connected.

The night would be extremely dark under the clouds – perfect for a stealth approach to the gang's camp on the canal. And if it rained, so much the better; they wouldn't be expecting any visitors, and their guard would be down. And in such extreme darkness, he might be able to get a little closer without being detected. Knowing that the occupants of the secret hideaway were armed with high-powered rifles struck a little fear into Ben, but he would rely on the darkness and the heavy timber on the island for his protection.

Twilight would come earlier than usual because of the overcast skies. Ben knew he had to find a logical spot on the backside of the island to land his boat, and make his way through the woods before total darkness set in, or he would never be able to locate the camp. Taking the canal by boat seemed too risky, as there was always the chance of some member of the gang arriving or leaving the camp.

The lagoon did have an outlet on the backside of the island – just a trickle of a stream no more than three feet wide and a foot deep came out of the woods about mid-way down the shoreline. Ben decided he'd hide the boat somewhere near and follow the stream inland. It should take him right to the camp, or at least close. He stuck the .22 pistol into his belt and put on his clear plastic rain jacket, certain that soon he would be getting wet.

By the time he had struggled along the muddy edge of the waterway for what seemed to be at least three or four hundred yards, total darkness was gobbling up everything visible. He thought he saw the flicker of a small light up ahead, and carefully felt his way up out of the ravine and onto the level, mud-caked dry ground, staring into the darkness and listening for any sounds. But now the light was no longer visible. That didn't seem so unlikely; the forest was quite dense, and the trees did an excellent job of blocking the view of anything that was any distance away – even a light.

Ben kept advancing slowly in the direction where he had seen the light, feeling his way from tree to tree. Here the ground was uneven, with deep pockets and ridges where the spring floodwaters had swirled and carved into the soil, making forward progress more difficult. More than once he fell to his knees as he stumbled over an unexpected drop-off. Ben was thankful that he had worn jeans instead of shorts.

Then the light appeared again just briefly, moving laterally, as if someone moving around in the camp was carrying a lantern. Ben determined that he had advanced quite some distance since he had first seen it, as it was much closer now. He pulled the .22 pistol from his belt and continued on, cautiously feeling the terrain with his foot before putting his whole weight into another step. He was soon within about thirty yards from where the light moved right to left, and this time he could make out the silhouettes and muffled voices of several people moving with it in a group.

Ben figured he was close enough for now, without putting himself in immediate danger. He lay prone on the ground, his heart beating a little faster than usual, wishing he had the binoculars to better see the activity. Never before had he known a dark-er night. The intense blackness seemed to close upon him like something tangible pressing against him, almost taking his breath away. He hadn't felt such anxious anticipation since the few moments just before his championship wrestling match.

A slight drizzle of rain had begun to fall, but that didn't seem to have much affect on the activity of the men in the camp. They continued with the methodical movement – right to left, then after numerous hollow-sounding footsteps and clamoring, back to the right. Now it appeared to Ben that one of the men seemed to be guiding the others with the lantern, and after some distance, they all disappeared into total blackness.

When they emerged again, moving to the left, Ben noticed a bit of lightning brighten the sky, followed by rolling thunder. A few moments later, another flash, much brighter this time, illuminated the area just enough to reveal a fair perspective of his location, and for Ben to get a very brief glimpse of the lagoon and the pontoon boat tied up at the bank, and the group of men that Ben thought consisted of at least six.

The pontoon. Of course. The movement of the men could only mean they were unloading more of the heavy crates like the ones he had seen them loading at the Fish Hatchery landing. But he couldn't determine where they were putting them. He waited for more lightning, and when it came he focused his attention in the direction where the men had disappeared before. He saw nothing but what appeared to be a dense thicket of brush. A couple of minutes passed, and then the sky opened up with a flash of lightning that lit the whole area bright as day for two or three seconds – long enough for Ben to get a good look at the brush again. It was then he realized that it was actually a well-disguised structure – a long, low building camouflaged much the same as the curtain hiding the entrance to the canal. Whatever the crates contained was being stored in that shack, and that shack was guarded like Fort Knox.

The rain was coming down harder, now. Ben flipped the hood of his rain gear over his head and hunkered down. He wondered if it was worth remaining there, as the storm would have more than likely driven all the men to seek shelter inside the little building.

Six men. Maybe more. And armed – greater odds than he cared to tackle alone. Being gunned down while taking an unnecessary risk would accomplish nothing. He decided to wait a little longer; maybe the rain would let up; maybe the men would leave on the pontoon; maybe his chances of getting a little closer would increase.

But as the time passed and the rain continued, Ben started to realize that he had probably accomplished as much as he would on this mission. He hadn't seen or heard any activity for more than an hour; the men had probably settled down in the hut for the night. This was, perhaps, the safest opportunity to retreat to his boat, where he could at least have some protection from the rain under the tarp that he always kept under the seat. There, he'd wait out the storm, and then he'd slip away before anyone knew he was on the island.

Sitting on the bare floor with his back to a wall in complete darkness, Erik went through the process of trying to keep up his spirits in the face of a gloomy outlook. Not only was he a prisoner in the hands of this band of Chicago thugs, but it also appeared that they suspected him of knowing their plans – which he didn't. At first, Erik had thought they were holding him until the police arrived to arrest him for trespassing, but now it was clear they had no intentions of turning him over to the law, as there had already been ample time for the Sheriff's Office to dispatch a deputy. What would happen next should prove interesting... but scary, as well.

He had never expected to gain access to the inside of this house; under the right circumstances, it may have been a step in the right direction, but whether or not he would ever have the opportunity to take advantage of the situation was quite uncertain. And even if he were able to escape from this awkward position, there was a good chance he would be hunted down like a wild animal.

By feeling around the walls, he had already discovered the small dimensions of the room, which was devoid of any furniture, and there was no light switch that he could find. There was a small window, though, overlooking the front yard, but with no moonlight, the room remained quite dark. He now knew why they had chosen this room for his detention – it would be impossible to jump from that window and survive the fall. He succeeded in opening the window, if only to let in a little fresh air, as it was getting quite stuffy and hard to breathe.

"What are you doing in there?" his guard demanded to know when he heard the window frame scraping as it opened.

"Just getting some air in here through the window," Erik responded.

That seemed to satisfy the man outside, and it was quiet again. Erik stretched his legs out across the floor and tried to relax. After some time, he noticed a faint light flickering on the wall opposite the window, and then it vanished. Just seconds later, he heard the distant rumble of thunder. And again, the light danced on the wall, but this time, he knew it was lightning, and the following growl came louder than before. Erik roused himself. A good thunderstorm had always appealed to him, and since sleep would be impossible, he went to the window. The horizon – across the river, he assumed – appeared intermittently as the lightning brightened the sky, revealing the ominous thunderheads. It seemed obvious that a considerable storm was brewing.

He had been standing there for at least ten minutes with his arms leaning on the windowsill as he watched the intensifying display, when he noticed the headlights of a car sweeping up the driveway. The black Lincoln Town Car stopped behind the others, and four men got out. Two came from the house to greet them, and then they all went inside.

It was definitely too late for a social party to start, so this must have been the gathering for some secret meeting. Erik longed to know what was going on downstairs, but with a locked door and an armed guard between him and the rest of the house, he might as well wish for the moon. Just then, the sky opened up with a flood of blue light, followed by a rather loud crash of thunder.

Erik saw something that sparked an idea in his head.

The window he was gazing from was in a dormer, and the lightning had revealed another similar dormer and window jutting out from the roof about thirty feet away. A crazy notion came to him to try to get to that other window. Such a feat, even in broad daylight might be risky, and a slip could mean a fall to sudden death. It may have been an act of lunacy, but Erik thought his future appeared quite dim, too, if he remained in that attic room until morning. So he resolved to try it. If he failed – well, it would be a quick ending. But if he succeeded, he might have a better chance to see the next sunrise. The approaching storm was his opportunity to take the risk he considered justified. He forced out all thoughts of failure – a psychological trick he had learned in his high school wrestling days – that had served him well on many occasions. It had to work here, too.

As soon as the next flash came, he quickly surveyed the steep roof below the window, and mentally marked its edge and the rain gutter, and then climbed through the small window, holding tightly to the sill and lowering his body until he was lying completely on the shingles and his feet searching for the gutter. He couldn't get his feet lodged satisfactorily in the gutter at first, and unconsciously he twisted his head around to look. At that very moment a blinding flash parted the heavens, illuminating the ground far beneath his feet as if it were the brightest day. And of course, the distance to the ground appeared much farther now than it had before. For a moment, the sight knocked his breath away. And while the thunder crashed and rolled, as if the sky were a wooden floor and giants were rolling ten pins with cannon balls, he lay on the steep slope with his eyes shut, his body trembling, while the thought of that awful drop gripped him like a nightmare.

He remained in that position for a long while, desperately attempting to regain his composure, and gradually his confidence returned, bringing with it new determination to succeed. He planted his toes in the rain gutter and slowly released his grip on the windowsill. He could only hope the gutter was sturdy, as he tried to support most of his weight on the roof. With utmost caution, he worked his way along the edge of the roof, and breathing a little prayer of thankfulness that his nerves had held, he grabbed the sill of the destination window. He pushed on the sash, but it was latched on the inside, just as the other one had been. But this was a small matter. He retracted his hand into the sleeve of his windbreaker, waited for a loud clap of thunder that would cover the sound of the breaking glass, and struck the bottom pane a sharp blow with his fist. Reaching inside, he freed the latch and pushed the window open. A hissing roar announced the approaching rain just as he pulled himself inside.

Once again, lightning brightened the tiny room he had entered, and Erik could see it was as bare as the one he left. He hoped the door wasn't locked from the outside. A sigh of relief came as he felt below the doorknob and found the old-fashioned skeleton key on the inside. He lingered a few moments to collect his thoughts and catch his breath, waiting for the next rumble of thunder to make his next move. No sooner than it had boomed out, he turned the knob and peeped through the crack that was just wide enough to let a cat in.

Less than thirty feet away sat his guard with his back toward Erik, reading a book under the light of a small lamp on the little table beside him. His revolver lay on the table, too, and Erik knew he would have to act quickly at the right moment. He waited, once again, for his friend, the thunder. With a half a dozen rapid strides he reached the man and caught him in a strangle hold that he knew would cause the man to quickly lose consciousness. He struggled fiercely for a few moments, but he stood little chance against Erik's advantage and powerful grip. He went limp and sank to the floor, motionless. Erik wondered what he should do to prevent the man from raising an alarm when he came to again, and he decided that locking him in the prison room was about the best he could do. He unlocked the door, dragged the man inside, closed the door and locked it again, and after examining the revolver that was loaded in all six chambers, he studied the hallway a few moments and turned out the light. Then he stole along the passage to the head of the stairs and stood listening.

All was quiet, so he descended to the next landing. His sneak-ers made not a sound on the steps. He could see there was a light on in the hallway below, and with the revolver ready he cautiously went down. He stopped near the bottom when he heard muffled voices coming from one of the downstairs rooms. At a pace slower than grass grows, he left the shelter of the stairwell and entered the hall. No one was there. Just a grandfather clock ticked steadily, pointing to one-thirty. The drone of conversation coming from a room behind a closed door down the hallway was the only other sound he could hear between the thunder booms. He tiptoed to the door, but this old house had such substantial oak doors, it was not possible to hear the words. Erik realized, once again, what a precarious position he was in – someone could appear at any moment. He glanced toward the front door where he had entered earlier. It was imperative that he should make not a sound getting to that door and outside as quickly as possible.

Once outside, his nylon windbreaker did little to protect him from the near torrential downpour that immediately drenched him to the skin, so it made little difference to remain and to con-tinue the surveillance. He couldn't get any wetter.

As he recalled, the house had no air conditioning, so that meant windows would be open, at least a little, even if it was rain-ing. Perhaps he would still be able to gather some information. There was no mistaking the room; it was the only one lit up, and it appeared as though the window was open a few inches at the bottom. At the risk of being seen in the light cast from the win-dow, Erik crept toward it, crouched down in a muddy flowerbed beneath it and listened.

Erik didn't recognize the cold, professional voice that was speaking inside the room. But it was quite distinct, and he could hear every word, despite the hiss of the rain.

"...New York has postponed the plan for ten days. That means we will carry out our procedure on September eleventh instead of the first."

There was a short lull, and other voices mumbled, but Erik couldn't make out the words. Then the distinctive voice spoke again: "I have checked the timetables – the *Delta Queen* is scheduled to arrive in La Crosse, late afternoon on that day, which means she will pass through these locks mid-morning. She is the oldest and most prestigious, the pride of their fleet, and she will be carrying a large number of passengers ... our most worthy objective." He paused for a moment, and then continued: "Well, we have our orders. It is all coordinated for the eleventh. Gentlemen... you have your instructions and you know what you must do by the tenth. Make sure the men on the island are alerted to the changes right away. With that, I will bid you farewell. It is a long drive back to Chicago... especially in this weather."

Erik heard a few mumbles and groans that made little sense. By then, the rain had lessened considerably. The meeting seemed to be breaking up, as Erik could hear chairs scraping the floor, papers shuffling, briefcases closing, footsteps and the heavy door opening. He had missed hearing the instructions that would have better explained what was going on, but there was nothing he could do about that now. He wondered how long it would be before they were aware of his absence. He had escaped unharmed, and he wasn't willing to take any more risks – the man on the third floor would surely soon alert the others of his escape. He'd had enough for one night. It seemed like a good time to depart for his car on Water Street.

He turned toward the back of the house to make his escape complete into the woods. There on the far edge of the yard he could see a shadow of a man lurking among the trees. It certainly wasn't one of the gang, Erik thought, or he would have already apprehended an intruder near the house. In an instant he made a decision to pursue the mystery person.

The rain had stopped completely now. He stole quietly from the deep obscurity of the house shadow and ran swiftly across the back yard. There was no fear in him now, only an overpowering curiosity as to who could be so interested in his movements about this place. He sped across the dark spaces toward the tall trees that rose between him and the town.

Already the unknown follower had taken flight. He had retreated to the edge of the woods and was hustling along a path that led toward the church. Erik had no intention to let this man escape without showing his face. Perhaps knowing who else was watching the activities of King and his gang would shed some new light.

Just past the church, Erik lunged forward, caught the man by his arm, and drew him to a halt.

"You don't get away that easy!" Erik called out, breathing heavily. "What are you doing out here?"

A shaft of light fell upon the man from a streetlamp. Erik was looking at a stranger whose appearance was nothing short of astonishing. From his floppy hat to his shabby boots, the man was clad in ragged, dirty plaid shirt and jeans. His face was dark and bearded; only the two eyes glaring at Erik revealed a creature that was actually alive.

"What were you after?" Erik barked. "Following me, were you?"

A second later Erik realized that he was looking at and speaking to one of those storybook characters he had often heard of but never seen – a hobo. If he had been near a tropical coast, this man would probably be called a beachcomber. What was the term he had heard used in these parts? *River rat?* A person who lives on the edge of civilization, picking the refuse he finds, begging when opportunity offers, and stealing when all else fails. Erik almost laughed. Surely this bum couldn't have any interest in the affairs of the King gang.

"I wasn't following you," the man said in a low tone.

"Then what were you up to?" Erik demanded.

The man's shaggy face turned nervously from side to side, as if seeking a path of escape. "You don't live here, either," he countered. "What were *you* up to?"

The response was totally unexpected, and Erik was caught speechless. He wiped the sweat from his forehead. "I suppose you were on a little mission of your own – stealing?"

The man's eyes flashed with sudden anger, but he didn't say another word.

"You'd better get out of here," Erik warned.

The scarecrow seemed relieved that Erik was allowing and

suggesting his getaway. He raised his hand in a sort of airy salute and shuffled off into the shadows of night.

Saturday August 18

Glad to see that both the limo and Ben's truck were parked in the driveway again, Troy knocked on the door once and let himself in. Sunday mornings were usually pretty quiet at Ben's place, anyway, but it seemed as though no one had been stirring at all, and it was nearly ten o'clock. He had stopped by just after midnight and found no one there, so he had just gone home to bed.

He went to the kitchen, started a pot of coffee brewing, and sat quietly at the table, wondering if he should go upstairs to Ben's room. But then he heard footfalls on the stairs, and then the bathroom door closed. A few minutes later, Ben strolled into the kitchen wearing only his underwear and a mildly surprised expression. "How long have you been here?" he asked Troy, and sat down at the table.

"Long enough to make coffee," Troy said. He got up to retrieve two cups from the cupboard, poured the coffee, and set a cup in front of Ben. "Anything else I can get for you, Hon?" he said, mocking the curly-haired waitress at the truck stop.

"Yeah," Ben replied, picking up on Troy's sarcasm. "I'll have a couple of eggs over easy, bacon and toast."

"Sorry. It's the cook's day off."

They both chuckled and sipped their coffee.

"Where were you guys last night?" Troy asked. "I stopped here around midnight... Erik's car and your truck were gone and the house was dark."

"It must've been after two when I got home, and I don't know when Erik came in. I thought you and Mandy went out last night."

"We did. But Mandy wasn't feeling good, so we came home right after the movie."

Erik joined them at the table after he poured himself a cup of coffee. "Ben, you're not gonna believe what happened to me last night," he said, his voice a little scratchy and eyes still puffy from just waking up.

Troy eyed the newcomer, also clad in just his underwear. "You look like you were out on an all-night drunk—"

"It wasn't that much fun! For starters, I got shot at."

Ben nearly choked on a swallow of coffee. "Shot at! Where? When? Are you okay? You're not hurt, are you?"

"No, I'm fine. It happened right here... down the driveway a little ways. It was just getting dark and I was gonna walk around for a while."

"They probably thought it was me," Ben said. "Did you see who it was?"

"No, but I found the getaway car later, just where I figured it would be."

"How do you know?"

"Because of the broken taillight." Erik went on to tell the entire episode of finding Lenny King's car, his imprisonment and escape at the old mansion in Genoa. "And then I heard them through an open window – some guy from Chicago was talking about some plan that came from someone in New York. Said it was all set for September eleventh... that the guys on the island should be notified right away. Oh, yeah! And then there was the part about the *Delta Queen*."

"What about the *Delta Queen*?" Ben said. His eyebrows had been raised during the entire story.

"He said the *Delta Queen* was scheduled to come through on the eleventh, and that she was a worthy objective, whatever that meant. What is the *Delta Queen*? A boat?"

"Yeah," Ben said. "It's an old paddlewheel steamboat... quite big... travels up and down the Mississippi with tourists... lots of 'em."

"What d'ya suppose he meant? Worthy objective."

"Well, my guess is that they're not planning a cruise," Ben said.

"Yeah, and then," Erik went on. "When I finally got out of there, I saw someone sneakin' around the back yard... near the edge of the woods."

"One of their people?"

"I thought so at first, but then I realized he wasn't coming after me. He was actually running away."

"So, what happened? Did you get a look at him?"

"Yeah. I caught him by the church."

"Who was it?"

"I didn't know him from a bundle of brooms. He was an older man with a beard and a tattered old hat... and his clothes were all ragged and dirty. I think he was just a bum looking for something to steal."

Ben and Troy glanced at each other. "Sounds like Frank," Ben said.

"Who's Frank?" Erik questioned.

"He's just an old river rat that lives in a shack down by the river. He's quite harmless, but it's kinda strange that he would be prowling around at that time of night."

When Ben was thoroughly convinced that Erik had not been hurt, he said, "Well, I had a little adventure last night, too."

"What did you do?"

"I went back out to the mystery island. Snuck up on their camp by the canal, but this time I went in from the other side of the island, and I got real close."

"So, what did you see?"

"It was too dark to see much detail, but in the lightning flashes, I saw them unloading more crates from the pontoon boat. And they've got a little building out there that's camouflaged quite well. I almost didn't see it. That's where they're storing those crates."

"How close did you get?"

"About thirty yards, but it started raining... hard... and there were about six of 'em, and y'know, they're heavily armed, so I didn't try to get any closer."

"Yeah...that was some tantoaster last night, eh?"

In unison, Troy and Ben said, "Tantoaster?"

Erik's eyes jumped from one to the other and back again with a questioning stare, as if they should understand his Maine slang. "Yeah... tantoaster. Y'know... Storm. I know it saved my ass... I'd never gotten out of that room alive if it hadn't been for the thunder covering the noise I made."

"Yeah… the lightning sorta lit up a few things for me, too," Ben said.

"Y'know what I think?" Troy said. "I think Erik should talk to Chet… see what he knows."

"Chet?" Erik had a puzzled look in his eyes. "Why would Chet know anything about any of this?"

"Because… before Stan canned him, he was getting kinda friendly with a couple of those drivers from Chicago. I think they hang out at the bar he goes to all the time."

"Yeah," Ben added. "I didn't think of that. And I *know* he'd never tell *me* anything."

Tuesday August 21

Ben had become quite disenchanted with the recent chain of events, and the fact that the police wouldn't listen to his plea made the whole situation more frustrating. Directly or indirectly, Peter Barrington was responsible for Stanley Hudson's disappearance through some devious actions, and he had gained control of Hudson Trucking through some underhanded, illegal proceedings, as well. Ben was certain of that. But he had not been successful in obtaining any proof positive. Whether or not Barrington was aware of the activities of Lenny King and his followers, or whether or not *they* had anything to do with Ben's father, Ben couldn't be sure. So far, Barrington had never been seen with them at any of the events that Ben, Troy, or Erik had witnessed, other than coffee shop get-togethers. Ben suspected it was quite likely that Peter was somehow at the center of it all.

He decided it was time for a confrontation with Peter Barrington. He knew Peter well enough to know that – if he could find him alone – Peter was not one to demonstrate violence on his own accord, and maybe a little bluffing might cause him to let something slip out.

It was a little past noon, and everyone except Barrington had left the office and warehouse for lunch. Ben walked into the building like he belonged there and started his search for Peter.

He wasn't hard to find. Outside the door to his office – the same office where Ben's father had spent so much time – Peter was just returning from the break room with a full cup of coffee. When he spotted Ben, his expression was not that of surprise, but rather of curiosity. "What brings you here, Ben?"

"We need to talk," Ben said.

"About what?"

"About my father."

"I've nothing to tell you that you don't already know, Ben."

"But I think you know where he is."

"I'm sorry, Ben. I don't."

"Then why are Lenny King and his goons trying to kill me?"

"What kind of nonsense are you talking about?"

"I'm talking about the time a while ago that Lenny shot at me, right outside this warehouse, and then his tribe chased me down with every intention of beating me to death."

"I don't know anything about—"

"And then the other night, they probably thought it was me they were shooting at again, right by my house. But it wasn't me."

Peter Barrington's expression turned to one of astonishment. Ben thought he was either putting on a very good act, or he really didn't know what his employees were doing behind his back.

"And what are they hauling out to that island with your pontoon boat?"

"I let them use my pontoon to go fishing. I don't know anything about any island."

"I think you're lying to me, Peter. What are all those late night gatherings at your house in Genoa all about? Surely you know about that."

"I let them use the river house any time they want. I suppose they have parties."

Ben's nerves, although he didn't realize it at that moment, were beginning to frazzle. The man's tone irritated him. Just then Ben heard the entrance door open behind him. He turned to see John Wolf enter. John had been in on the chase and the attempted beating.

"John," Barrington said, his attitude abruptly changed now that he had some backup. "John, will you please show this young man out?"

John approached and started to grab Ben's arm, as if to physically escort him to the door. Ben jerked away quickly and being of superior strength and defensive capabilities, retaliated with an aggressive push, slamming John against a wall. "Didn't you learn the last time out in the parking lot?" Ben said, his words having the affect of a carefully tossed grenade. His anger was getting difficult to control as he kept Wolf pinned. "Maybe you need a little reminder." And with that he connected a right fist squarely on Wolf's jaw with a tremendous blow. John Wolf sank to the floor and offered no more resistance. Peter Barrington stood there, knowing it would be foolish to attempt any further physical confrontation with a powerhouse like Ben. He just backed away toward his office door.

Ben realized he had made an unwise choice to even come there. He stared at Barrington a long moment, then turned and went to the door. It was best, he thought, to get away from there as quickly as possible before any more of King's gang returned from lunch.

He drove his pickup out into the country to calm his nerves and to get his thoughts together about the serious issues facing him now. He needed to clear his head and make some decisions regarding his own future. Maybe it would be best for him, he thought, to just go back to Colorado, get back into his old job there, and try to work his way through to his engineering degree. He didn't want to sell his house – that was his security blanket if things didn't work out in Colorado. His little brother could look after it for him, and he already had a built-in tenant – Erik. Erik seemed quite responsible, and his job with Bert Greer had turned out much better than he had expected. Ben thought he'd have to come up with a tactful way to tell Erik that he'd soon be paying full rent.

After a half-hour of just aimlessly driving through the country and thinking, Ben headed back toward home. He turned into his driveway and saw the city police car parked in front of the house.

The limo was there, too, so he knew Erik was at home.

Ben thought quickly. Obviously, Peter Barrington had notified the police of what would surely be called an assault on John Wolf, and an officer was there to question him about the incident. Should he willingly walk in and confront the issue? He would be truthful in saying that he acted in self-defense, although he had no witness to back him up, and perhaps he had reacted a little more harshly than had been necessary.

Just minutes before, he had determined to accept the hard knocks that life was dishing out to him, and try to move forward. But now, another obstacle had jumped out. He wasn't sure that he should take the chance to be arrested and detained. Maybe if he could postpone that risk for a while, he could contact Erik sometime later and find out why the officer had been there – simply to ask questions, or to make an arrest.

He backed out of the driveway, turned toward town and drove away. He would take the back roads to La Crosse. It was easy enough to stay out of sight in a city that big, and he could call Erik from there. Keeping ever alert, he noticed Lenny King's Dodge Intrepid leaving the Hudson Trucking lot, and it seemed, right then, that pursuit by that faction was a bigger risk than by the police. He made a quick left turn onto a side street, and followed a serpentine route across town to a country road heading west. He knew plenty of off-road trails where his four-wheel-drive could easily lose a passenger car, but a mile out of town, passing over several rolling hills and dales, it was difficult to tell if a car was following.

Then, the unthinkable happened – the right front tire of Ben's truck went flat. It had been punctured by a sharp piece of metal in the road causing a very abrupt loss of air. Ben pulled the truck off onto a dirt roadway into a farmer's field. No sooner had he inspected the flat tire than he realized there was no spare; it was in the garage at home. Getting to La Crosse would not be an easy task now.

He sat down in the shade of the truck, leaning against the flat tire. If he relaxed a few minutes, he could think more clearly. But that lasted about as long as a clean shirt would last in mud wrestling. He was near the point of panic. For the past few weeks he had practiced the Christian virtue of patience, but he had been forced to deal with so many people who lived on the edge of right and wrong, and now his patience was wearing so thin he could see right through it. His life had turned into a miserable mess of vague facts and hard feelings that he was trying to face and couldn't. It was like trying to grasp something in the dark and not knowing what shape or size the thing was.

Then he heard the growl of a diesel engine and the hum of truck tires approaching from the east. It was a lumberyard delivery truck, and perhaps a low risk source for a ride. Ben sprinted to the edge of the road, and the driver of the truck slowed to a stop in response to his distressful wave.

"Got a little problem with my pickup... flat tire and no spare," Ben explained to the driver. "Wondering if you could give me a lift."

"Well, I'm headed to the north side of La Crosse. Where do you need to go?"

"La Crosse is fine," Ben replied. He opened the door and climbed into the passenger seat.

When the truck was rolling again, the middle-aged driver, quite chubby and whose company uniform made him look like a well-dressed sand bag turned to Ben and said, "Where in La Crosse d'ya want to go?"

Ben hesitated as he tried to think of some unlikely place where he could disappear for a while. He turned and peered out the rear window of the truck cab. Lenny King's car was stopped beside the road at his pickup and two men were getting out, perhaps anticipating to find Ben somewhere nearby on foot. He could only assume they had not seen him get into the lumberyard truck, as they didn't seem in a hurry to give chase. Luck would have to be on his side, Ben thought, to gain enough of a lead before his pursuers realized how he had evaded them.

"I'm getting back pretty early," the driver went on. "I'm in no hurry and I could drop you off most anywhere... I mean it's not like I have to catch a train or anything."

That gave Ben an idea. "Well, as a matter of fact," he said, slouching down in the seat. "I do. If you're going anywhere near the train depot…"

"Sure… we'll go right by it. I can drop you off there."

That would be a good place to be out of sight. No one would think of looking for him at the depot. He was beginning to feel like a fleeing felon, and he was afraid his nervousness was showing. He had to calm himself down. "I work for a big construction company… out in Colorado," Ben said, trying to strike up some friendly conversation. "I drive a delivery truck, too."

The driver just nodded and didn't offer any reply. He appeared to have the personality of a potato, so Ben didn't attempt any further conversing. All during the rest of the ride through La Crosse, he just sat quietly watching the scenery go by. As promised, the driver turned his truck off Rose Street and followed the Amtrak signs to the depot parking lot. "Here we are," he said dryly. "Have a nice trip."

"Thanks," Ben said. "I really appreciate the ride." He swung the door open, jumped out, pushed the door shut again, and watched the truck pull away.

It must have been a light travel day for the railroad as there were just a few cars in the parking lot and no people moving about. A La Crosse city police car cruised slowly by, and although Ben was certain they would not be on the lookout for him yet, there remained the possibility that his description had been circulated, and it wasn't worth the risk of staying out in the open – even if that risk was slim. He turned and walked toward the depot at a normal pace so as not to draw attention.

Inside the old building, he saw a timetable of arrivals and departures on the wall next to the ticket office window. The next arrival wasn't due for several hours, and that might explain the lack of activity at the moment. He headed for the pay phone sign above the door that led into another room, dug in his pocket for some change, and thought about what he would tell Erik in the limited amount of time of the toll call. But he only heard the answering machine. He explained his truck's location, and that Erik and Troy should get his spare tire from the garage, change the tire and drive the truck home. He didn't say where he was at the present time, but that he would call again later.

He sat on one of the waiting room benches, attempting to formulate a plan. It probably wasn't safe to return home right away, as King and his men would certainly be watching and waiting for another opportunity to strike.

A half hour had passed when he noticed through the front windows the maroon Dodge that stopped in the depot parking lot. How could they have known to come here? Ben thought. The lumberyard truck driver – they must have seen the truck and had talked to the driver at the lumberyard.

Ben jumped to his feet and hurried to the station door facing the tracks. Outside to the left he knew there was a narrow paved roadway along the tracks that led right to *Bucky's Burger Barn*. He made a run for it, hoping he could be away before King and his companion entered the depot. If they didn't see him there, perhaps they would think he had left by train, and they would give up the chase.

Too late for the lunch bunch and too early for Happy Hour, *Bucky's* was far from being crowded. Only a dozen or so customers gathered in a few small groups at tables, and a couple of thirty-something construction workers sat gulping down their burgers and fries at the bar near the entrance. A Tiger Woods golf match on the big screen TV didn't command a great deal of attention.

What could be considered a "neighborhood bar," *Bucky's* offered a great place for sports-minded people to hang out for a few beers and informal dining. Its NASCAR theme that started on the outside with a mock racecar on the roof was carried to the interior with hundreds of scale model racecar replicas in Plexiglas cases lining the walls. From the ceiling hung pseudo street signs with names of famous racecar drivers – Dick Trickle Blvd, Harry Gant Avenue, Alan Kulwicki Drive, and Davy Allison Road.

Ben quickly found his way to a stool at the far end of the bar. He nervously scanned the whole place. He'd been there many times with Troy – although not recently – but he felt the need to re-familiarize himself with the layout and the path past the pool table to the rear exit, if that became necessity. He was relieved to see a familiar face behind the bar.

"Hi, Charlie," Ben said as the bartender approached.

Charlie recognized the face, but he couldn't recall Ben's name.

"How ya doin,'" he responded. "Haven't seen you for a long time."

"Okay, I guess," Ben replied. He glanced toward the front entrance nervously a couple of times. "I've been in Colorado at college. That's why I haven't been around."

"Oh, yeah," Charlie laughed. "Now I remember... you're the wrestling champ. You used to come in here with Troy."

Ben gave a half smile to the jovial bartender. "That would be me."

"I still see Troy in here now and then," the bartender added.

Ben jerked his head toward the entrance when the door opened. A gray-haired man entered and sauntered over to the bar.

Charlie laid a menu in front of Ben and then started to draw a tap beer for the new arrival. Ben briefly studied the menu. "I'll have a Southwestern and a *Coke*," he told Charlie.

Charlie gave a nod. He delivered the order to the kitchen and returned with a red can and an ice-filled glass. He discretely examined Ben's face – as a bartender he had learned the art of reading faces, and he detected distress. "Is something wrong?" he asked. "You look kinda worried."

Ben stared at the bartender for a long moment. Charlie wasn't exactly a close friend. It was really none of his business. But then, maybe it wouldn't hurt to seek some advice from an outside source. He sipped the *Coke* to moisten his dry mouth. Softly, he spoke, "The men who probably killed my dad are after me, too. I just gave them the slip over at the train depot."

Charlie's cheerful smile slowly turned to a blank stare as the information soaked in. "Should I call the police?"

Ben thought quickly. A policeman was the last person he wanted to talk to right then. "No. The cops won't do anything, and those guys would've been here by now if they were still on my trail."

"Why can't the police help?"

"It's a long story, Charlie. Trust me."

"Well, is there anything I can do to help?"

Ben shrugged his shoulders and shook his head. "I doubt it."

"So… what are ya gonna do?"

"Well, I can't go home, so I don't know."

"You got money for a motel? There's one just up the street."

Ben thought a moment and nodded. A motel would probably be the safest place to hide away for the night. He had a little cash, but there was a *Visa* card in his wallet just for emergencies, and this certainly qualified.

"Tell ya what," Charlie said. "I'll be off work in twenty minutes. I can give you a lift if you want."

Ben wasn't one to impose inconvenience on anyone. He shrugged his shoulders as an indication of uncertainty.

"It's no trouble," Charlie assured. "I'm going that way anyway. I can drop you off. Really. It's no trouble at all."

"Well, okay.   Can I get that burger to go?"

The *Econo Lodge* was only a five-minute ride away. Charlie knew the back streets and avoided some of the rush-hour traffic. "Is there anything else I can do to help?" he asked as he turned his car off Rose Street and came to a stop at the motel front entrance.

Ben shook his head and forced a friendly smile. "No, Charlie. You've been a big help already." He swung open the passenger door and added, "I really appreciate your friendship… even though you don't know me very well."

Charlie returned a worried sort of grin. "Glad to be of assistance, Champ."

With the clunk of the closing door and the muffled engine roar, Ben realized that he was probably waving good-bye to the last friendly face he would see that day. As he stood there alone, he felt a little smile creep onto his face. No one had called him *Champ* in a long time, and even he had put all that behind. There had been a time when he thrived on the recognition – the attention, mostly.   He loved it when anyone admired his well-proportioned muscular form, or stared at the eagle tattooed on his left shoulder, visible only when he was shirtless. But in time, that all seemed more a nuisance, and he began to consider his past accomplishment as just good, solid preparation that gave him the ability to stay focused. Every now and then, something would remind him – like Charlie had just done – and he would bask in a brief moment of reflected glory, remembering how proud he had felt whenever someone called him "Champ." But he wasn't the champ anymore. Someone else had claimed the title the following year, and Ben honorably relinquished the invisible crown to his successor.

Now he was exiling himself to the confines of a motel room where he would take advantage of the time by logically thinking things out. He turned and started for the door with the white box containing his dinner in hand.

By the time he was checked into the room, his burger and fries were cold. And what was worse, to get to the microwave in the area where the continental breakfast was served, he'd have to pass by the front desk and the girl who was way too inquisitive as to why he had no luggage. Ben wasn't quite sure if she had accepted his story about *Amtrak* losing his bags, but at least his driver's license confirmed the Colorado home address he had used when he checked in. Luck was with him this time, as the curious girl at the desk was occupied with some more check-ins when he came down the stairs, and she didn't even notice him.

Ben propped both pillows up against the headboard, kicked off his shoes and leaned back on them with the warmed over burger in his lap. As much as he'd like to relax and basically forget about the rest of the world just for one evening, he knew that was not likely. He had been over all the details in his mind a hundred times, searching for a single clue that might lead him to his missing father. There had to be something he had overlooked.

He thought about that morning in Colorado when Bryan had called him on the phone. His brain immediately focused on the brief conversation he'd had with Peter Barrington just a short time later. There had never been any doubt in Ben's mind that Peter was the key player in Stan Hudson's vanishing act. His dad had indicated in several letters that they had had numerous disagreements, and Ben could think of no one with a better motive than Peter to do him harm.   But the sheriff insisted that Peter was clean, and that he had found no physical evidence of any wrongdoing.   And so far, neither had Ben.   Frustration levels were high, but not nearly as high as his suspicions of Peter Barrington.

But then Ben thought about Grandpa Ernest and the chicken gravy theory. Maybe he was dipping his spoon in the wrong bowl. Maybe there was a chance that Peter *didn't* know about all the strange activities carried on by his drivers. And maybe those activities appeared as something completely different than they actually were.

It seemed obvious to Ben that Lenny King and his band of followers were using his dad's trucking company for purposes other than taking care of freight customers. Surely, Peter had to be aware of that, but he didn't seem concerned that the business would suffer lasting consequences.   If that didn't matter to him, then the only answer had to be that he had been drawn into such an irresistible financial deal – one that Stanley Hudson had adamantly opposed – that gave someone else control of operations. The multi-million-dollar negotiations that Stan had mentioned in his letters didn't concern transportation of freight at all. It simply gave control of the company to a third party without drawing any outside attention.

Although purely speculation, Ben thought it seemed a logical explanation for *why* Stan Hudson, the only opposing factor, had to be removed. With that came the question: who had removed him? It seemed reasonable that Lenny King – whoever he was – possessed equal, or perhaps more motivation to make that happen. Perhaps his incentives were on a much larger scale. The meeting that Erik and Troy had overheard at the river cottage that night several weeks ago had vaguely revealed someone in New York might be involved. And at Central Express Erik had heard a couple of the drivers mention something about trucks running empty to North Carolina, and returning to Chicago with loads so light that they would never be scrutinized at any weigh station.

Now it made more sense why King was constantly pursuing him. King probably suspected that Ben's father had revealed what he knew to Ben, or that Ben had somehow discovered the secrets of King's operation. Oh, how Ben wished that were true. "Whatever King is hiding, it's worth killing for," Ben mumbled. And as soon as the words had left his lips, his brow furrowed with disgust, ashamed that he could even suggest his father was dead. He'd chastised his brother for saying it, and now he, himself, had fallen victim to the gruesome thought.

He wanted to put the matter out of his mind for a while because it was all too disturbing. He got up from the bed, walked into the bathroom, and splashed cold water onto his face. In the mirror he stared at his own image that showed a strange mix of worry and relief – worry that he may never learn the truth, and relief that he might be coming to terms with the probability of his father's death.

Searching his thoughts for some sort of temporary diversion, he remembered seeing some magazines on a table down in the lobby. Unconcerned about the curious girl at the front desk, he raced down the stairs and quickly found the table with the magazines. Like the periodicals found in almost any waiting room, they weren't the most current issues, but right then, anything would do. Ben grabbed an old issue of *Newsweek* and headed back to his room.

After merely paging through a good portion of the publication, not really reading but instead scanning the headlines and pictures, he came across something that caught his eye. It was an article telling the "inside scoop" on CIA and FBI investigations of the February 26, 1993 World Trade Center bombing. The article was quite comprehensive with details about tracking the bomber, and how the thirty technicians assigned to TRADE-BOM, as the FBI had dubbed the investigation, working in shifts around the clock had come up with the evidence to identify him. Ben was quite intrigued with the story and kept reading. It told of how the investigators identified a Ryder rental van by the vehicle identification number found on twisted wreckage of an axle while sifting through rubble at the blast zone. They had traced the van to a rental agency in Jersey City, and as a bonus, the staff there informed FBI agents that Mohammed Salemeh, the man who had rented the van, had reported the vehicle stolen, was obtaining a police report, and was to return in a couple of days to collect his security deposit. When he did, the FBI was waiting for him.

The magazine article contained many pictures related to the event, and photos supposedly taken secretly inside a terrorist training camp in Afghanistan depicting known Islamic terrorists that may have been connected to the bombing. Ben studied the pictures. He could feel the wickedness piercing into him from the eyes of those men. One in particular grabbed his attention. The caption identified one of the individuals in the photo as Imad al-Karim, current whereabouts, unknown. Ben's eyes widened. The man in the picture seemed strangely familiar.

It had been a long, stressful day. Ben lay back on the bed and closed his burning eyes. He wanted to call home, but he thought it would be best to wait until later, giving Erik and Troy plenty of time to change the flat tire on his truck and get it back to the house. Desperately he hoped they had found it unharmed.

When he awoke abruptly to the sound of loud voices in the hall outside his door, it took him a few long moments to remember where he was, and why he was there. The lamp beside the bed lit the room brightly, but when he pulled a curtain slightly aside and peered out the window, he discovered darkness had veiled the city. He squinted at his watch. It was nearly 10:30 PM. He reached for the phone and dialed his number.

A familiar voice answered, "Hello?"

"Erik! Are you alone?"

"Ben… where are you?"

"Are you alone?" Ben repeated emphatically.

"No. Troy's here with me. We just got your truck back a little while ago."

"Is anybody else there?"

"No. Why?"

"I saw a city squad car by the house today… I thought they might be looking for me."

"Ben, what's wrong? Where are you?"

"Well? Were they looking for me?"

"No. Bob stopped by to talk to me about a fender bender I witnessed in the street by the shop. He never asked about you. Why would he be looking for you?"

"Cause I got in a little scuffle with one of Barrington's guys today at the warehouse. Have you seen any of them hangin' around?"

"No... I don't think so. Are you okay?"

"Yeah, and thanks for getting my truck. Is it okay?"

"Yeah, it's fine. Not a scratch. Ben, what's wrong? Where are you?"

"I'll tell you where I am as soon as I'm sure there's no one else there."

"Here... talk to Troy. Maybe you'll believe him." Erik handed the receiver to Troy.

"Hey, Ben. We've been kinda worried about you."

"Are you guys alone?"

"Yeah, Ben. There's nobody else here. It's just me and Erik. What happened? Where are you?"

"I'm... I'm at a motel in La Crosse."

"What happened, Ben? Why are you there?"

"It's a long story, Troy."

"Well, can't you give me a short version?"

"Okay. First, I thought the cops were looking for me because I decked one of King's buddies over at the warehouse."

"As far as I know, the cops aren't looking for you, Ben. But why did you –?"

"Well, then King followed me out of town, and I just barely got away after the tire went flat on my truck... caught a ride just before he showed up."

"Lucky. So, how did you end up in a motel in La Crosse?"

"Charlie at the *Burger Barn* gave me a lift to the *Econo Lodge* up on Rose Street."

"Charlie?"

"Like I said, Troy. It's a long story."

"Should we come pick you up?"

"Tomorrow. The room's paid for. I might as well stay here tonight. Besides... it's late."

"Ben? Are you okay? You sound a little ragged."

"I'm fine... just a little tired and stressed out. That's all."

"Okay. I'll come and get you about ten tomorrow morning."

"Hey... Troy?"

"Yeah..."

"Thanks. I... I..."

"It's okay. Get some sleep. I'll see you in the morning."

Wednesday August 22

Ben pulled out the magazine that he hid under his shirt as soon as he sat down in the passenger seat of Troy's Buick. Troy just sat there behind the wheel staring at him, not making any movements to put the car in motion. Ben appeared as if he had not slept.

"You look awful," Troy said. "Your clothes are a mess. You didn't sleep last night, did you?"

Ben just stared straight ahead through the windshield. "Not much," he mumbled.

"Did you even take a shower this morning?"

"No."

"Ben, what happened yesterday?"

"I told you what happened... on the phone last night."

"Well there must be something you're not telling me 'cause you sure aren't yourself today."

Ben slid down in the seat. He rolled his head to the left on the backrest and made eye contact with Troy. "I think I might've discovered something last night," he said with a trembling voice. "I don't know exactly what to make of it, but I'll show you when we get home."

Troy saw the exhaustion on every inch of his friend's being. Home probably was the best place for him right now. He started the car, backed away from the parking space and headed toward the street. Forty-five minutes later he shook Ben's shoulder to wake him up as they pulled into Ben's driveway. "Think you can walk into the house, or do I need to carry you?" Troy joked.

Ben's eyes opened slowly, and it took a few seconds for him to get oriented into his current surroundings. He stared for a long moment at his pickup truck parked in front of the garage, and then he remembered why he wasn't driving it. "Thanks for getting my truck home," he said to Troy, got out of the car and staggered to where he expected to see a dusty black rim and tire. But instead, the shiny, polished aluminum wheel stared back at him, just as it usually did.

"Oh yeah! Erik fixed your tire already," Troy announced. "We took it right to his shop last night and did it."

They both ambled into the house where Ben immediately plopped down on the sofa. Troy sat beside him. "Okay. What is it you're gonna show me?"

Ben gazed into Troy's eyes questioningly, as if the request were a total mystery. Then he blinked, shook his head and looked down at the magazine he was still clutching in his hand. He opened it up to the bombing investigation article and handed it to Troy, pointing to a particular photo. "Look at this picture. Who do you see in the background?"

Troy scanned over the open pages and then focused on the picture that Ben pointed out. It appeared to be a mountainous desert setting with several rugged, angry men, all poised with assault rifles. He zeroed in on the one man in the background. "I don't know. Am I supposed to know who this is?" Then he read the caption that named all the men in the photo. Struggling a little with the pronunciation he said, "Imad al-Karim. Why should I know who this is?"

"Look real close," Ben said.

Troy studied the photo some more. The man in question did look vaguely familiar, but Troy thought it was only because Ben had suggested he was familiar.

"That's Lenny King," Ben said.

Troy held the magazine out at arm's length and focused on the image again.

"It's him... only younger. According to the article, that photo was taken ten or fifteen years ago in Afghanistan... at a terrorist training camp."

Troy kept staring at the face. "I don't know. I guess it *could* be him. But if it is, what's he doing here... now?"

"Good question," Ben replied. "I'm just not thinking too clearly right now."

Troy laid the magazine on the coffee table and grabbed Ben's wrist, urging him to get up. "C'mon... let's get you into the shower. You'll feel better. And while you're doing that, I wanna read the rest of this article."

The article was quite interesting, Troy thought, but he wasn't thoroughly convinced that the picture, although a strong resemblance, was of Lenny King. It just didn't seem logical that someone who had trained as a militant in a foreign country would be working as a truck driver in Wisconsin. Ben's imagination was probably getting the best of him. He had certainly been under a lot of stress lately.

When Ben sauntered back to the living room after the long, refreshing shower, he sat next to Troy on the couch, still rubbing his wet hair with a towel. "I'm gonna talk to Sheriff Lowery," he said.

Troy tossed the magazine on the coffee table. The shower had apparently revived Ben, but he hated the thought of Ben heading off into another tunnel of disappointment. "Why don't you wait 'til tomorrow, after you've have a good night's sleep and you're thinking a little clearer?"

"I'm thinking just fine," Ben snapped. "I'm going today."

Troy said nothing more. There seemed little need in arguing a point he couldn't win. Nor did it matter. He went to the kitchen to make a pot of coffee.

Ben sat in his truck in the Sheriff's Department parking lot for several minutes just thinking about how he would word the questions and the presentation of his new-found information. So far, throughout this entire ordeal, he had found himself a little disappointed with the response from the sheriff and his deputies. He fully understood that there was just so much they could do, but he also thought they had given up the search for Stan Hudson much too soon. Until now, he had always directed his suspicions toward Peter Barrington, which had produced no results among the lawmen. But now he had strong indications that Lenny King could have had interest in eliminating his father. If he could convince the sheriff that King might have some skeletons in his closet, perhaps the investigation would find some new direction.

But there was also the matter of the little scuffle he had had with John Wolf at the warehouse, and whether or not it was reported to police. It could find him in the midst of trouble he didn't need. His apprehension overpowered him briefly, but then he picked up the magazine, stepped out of the truck and started on the sidewalk for the office door. If his theory was correct, Lenny King and his men had something to hide, and they would probably avoid contact with any lawmen.

Inside he asked for the sheriff, and because everyone there knew him and was aware of the circumstances, he was directed to the sheriff's private office down the hallway. The door was open, and Sheriff Lowery sat at his desk sorting through a stack of papers. He noticed Ben standing silently in the doorway, smiled pleasantly, and greeted his visitor, "Hello, Ben."

"Hello, Sheriff," Ben answered with an air of confidence. He took a couple of steps inside the room as the sheriff rose from behind his desk and extended a friendly handshake.

"Good to see you again," Sheriff Lowery said. "What brings you here?"

"I…" Ben hesitated. "I wanted to talk to you about my dad."

"I figured that much," said the sheriff. "Have you heard from him?"

"No. And I guess I can assume that because I haven't heard from you, you haven't, either."

Sheriff Lowery's smile melted away. "No, Ben, we haven't." He directed Ben to sit in a chair beside the desk. "Will you be able to return to school this fall?"

Ben shrugged his shoulders. "I don't know… depends on whether Dad… I mean… well, I just don't know."

"I know this must be tough for you, Ben. I hope you realize we've done all we can."

"Well, that's kinda what I wanted to talk to you about. I know that I've always had some strong feelings about Peter Barrington..."

"Yes, Ben, I know you suspect he has everything to do with your missing father—"

"But I've found something else," Ben interrupted. "How much do you know about Lenny King?"

The sheriff squinted as if taxing his memory. "Oh... do you mean *Leonard* King? One of Peter's drivers?"

"Yes."

"Why do you ask?"

Ben hoisted the magazine onto the desk. "Well, for starters, I found his picture in this old *Newsweek*." He flipped the pages, quickly located the article, and turned it so it was facing the sheriff. Then he pointed to the picture of the man he thought was a dead ringer for Lenny King.

Lowery perused the pages. "Yes, I remember reading this article. I have a subscription." He studied the photo that Ben had pointed out. "And what makes you believe this is King?"

"Well, it looks just like him, and King does have a peculiar accent."

"Ben, I personally interviewed all those guys, including Leonard King." The sheriff opened a desk drawer and for a few seconds appeared to be searching for something. Finally he pulled out a thick file folder that contained many sheets of paper. It looked as if it had been handled a lot. He held it up so Ben could see a typewritten label on the folder tab: HUDSON, STANLEY. "If you think we didn't thoroughly investigate your father's case, Ben, here's all my notes and information we gathered." While he spoke, he paged through the sheets and stopped when he found the one he wanted. "Here's the info on Leonard King." Using his index finger he traced over the lines of notes. "He came to Chicago from New York and went to work for Peter Barrington as a truck driver. We checked his background records in both Chicago and New York, and other than a couple of traffic tickets in New York, he appears to be clean. There's no other police records on him."

"Well, I know from personal experience," Ben said, "that Lenny King is not a very nice person."

"Sorry, Ben, but police records don't always indicate *nice*. And as for that picture in *Newsweek*... I'm sure there are a lot of people who might look like that guy."

Ben flinched with the startling ring of the phone that sounded like an electronic cricket. The sheriff picked up the receiver and put it to his ear. "Hello..." A long pause followed. "Yes... I can be there in about half an hour," he said and hung up the phone. He stood and looked into Ben's eyes. "I'm sorry, Ben, but I have to leave – an urgent matter I have to attend to." He reached to the end of the desk, grasped his gun belt and began strapping it around his waist. "You take care of yourself, and I'll let you know if I learn anything new... okay?" With that he escorted Ben out into the hallway and hurried to the dispatcher's desk.

Once again, Ben thought it seemed as though the sheriff had used the phone call as an excuse to exit from their conversation. It occurred to him, too, that his frustrations were caused not only by his vanished father, but also that he was finding great difficulty in convincing anyone that Lenny King was, perhaps, a dangerous threat to society. Ben decided to just go home.

Troy sat at the kitchen table with a cup of coffee. "So, did you get to talk to the sheriff?" he asked when Ben walked in the door.

After a long pause Ben replied in a forlorn voice, "Yeah."

Troy knew without asking that there had not been a great deal of success. "So, what did he have to say?"

Ben poured himself a cup of coffee and sat down at the table. "He's not the least bit interested... says he checked out King's police record, and there's nothing on him." He took a sip of the coffee. "Then he went rushing off before I could tell him anything else. Guess he didn't want to talk to me any more."

"Well, Ben, you've got to admit – it's purely speculation, and it *is* kind of a long shot in the dark."

"I'm not so sure about that, Troy. All the strange things that are happening, and the fact that there was no mention of the fight I had with Wolf yesterday means they didn't report it, which means they don't want any contact with the police."

"So, what does that prove?"

"It proves that they don't want any attention drawn to them, and whatever it is they're doing out on that island."

The conversation fell into silence while Troy got up from his chair to retrieve the coffee pot. He refilled both cups and returned to his seat. Ben's point was undisputable, and he could only agree that recent events did seem a little bizarre. Recollections of some of the adventures raced through his mind: heavily armed men guarding a hidden lagoon on that island; Erik kidnapped and held prisoner in Barrington's river house, barely escaping and... That reminded Troy of something else. "Didn't Erik mention a date that he'd overheard them talking about that night they caught him and locked him in the attic?"

Ben's eyebrows rose. "Yeah." He thought a long moment. "I think he said September eleventh. Yes. I'm sure of it."

"Okay. That means we have until September *tenth* to find some proof of what they're doing, and maybe convince somebody to do something about it."

"You're right. We know *when* they're gonna do whatever they're planning..."

"But we don't know what," Troy added.

Ben strained in deep thought. "The answer is on that island. Feel like another camping trip on the river?"

"Sure. But it's getting close to the end of August. I have to get moved back to my room in La Crosse in a few days. I go back to school the first week in September, y'know."

"Okay. Let's see if Erik can take off a few days and we'll go this weekend."

Thursday August 23

Another camping trip to the river had been on Erik's mind ever since he returned home from his first. It didn't bother him that a little risk might be involved when Ben and Troy explained the real reason for the voyage. Facing elements of danger, he had gained considerable confidence in himself over the course of the summer. The adventures he had experienced were beginning to make him feel like a soldier of fortune, although he wasn't exactly sure what a soldier of fortune was *supposed* to feel like. He kept that little secret to himself.

"Erik," Ben said as they began planning the trip that evening. "I know I've been the cause for you to find yourself in some rather dangerous situations, and I'm sorry for that. If you have any second thoughts about going back out there…"

"Don't be silly," Erik responded instantly. "I'm happy as a clam at high tide. And I'd be mighty pissed off if you went without me."

"Okay," said Ben. "Troy and I can get all the stuff ready tomorrow while you're at work."

"There's only a shovel-full of work for me at the shop tomorrow," Erik replied. "I don't think Bert will mind at all if I leave early. I'll be back here by ten."

Friday August 24

As usual, Ben was up and working out long before any of the others were awake. He heard the limo start and watched Erik turn out of the driveway heading up the road into town. With good reason, he admired Erik. He knew of few people like him, woven with such strong fibers of alliance, and he was thankful that Erik played on his team. For a brief while, Ben reminisced about his own school days at Westby High and how he had made the Norsemen athletic department a proud group. His focus had always been on wrestling and football; he was a natural for both. As a popular jock, though, he was drawn into social circles he didn't desire, and was often forced to graciously reject invitations into unwanted relationships. But he enjoyed the attention from girls and guys at the time, and so it had created a difficult time for him because he felt almost obligated to honorably accept those friendships, even though he knew they were just seeking a status symbol. His teammates were his social circle, and he had Troy who had stayed by his side since childhood. Unlike the others, Troy's friendship was sincere, and not just because Benjamin Hudson had become a state champion. And now, Troy was still there when the others were not.

And then along had come Erik, who somehow changed Ben's outlook. In quiet, private conversation, Erik had told him of his life back in Maine. He couldn't make claim to any success: although he was a strong athlete, he had never captured any titles, and he shamefully admitted that his family and friends had openly ridiculed his near misses. His confidence – back in Maine – had been shattered, and being constantly reminded of what his fellow schoolmates chose to call failure, he was driven to abandon all self-esteem. Adding insult to injury, his only real friend was killed in a car accident on graduation night. It was enough to break the spirit of any young boy.

But here he was, a thousand miles from home, eager to keep trying for acceptance. He knew he couldn't erase the past. His attitude, though, of putting all the bad stuff behind and moving forward made him admirable in Ben's eyes. Ben knew it had just been chance that landed Erik in this small Midwestern town. He hadn't come looking for anyone in particular, and in the short time he had lived here, he was definitely showing genuine characteristics. Ben knew they would be friends for a long time.

When Erik's Mustang rolled in the driveway at 10:30, Ben was just hooking the boat trailer to his truck. None of the camping gear was loaded yet, and Troy was nowhere in sight. Erik pulled the Mustang into the garage where Ben's truck usually sat, and where the Mustang would stay for the duration of the camping trip.

"Where's Troy?" he asked. He noticed that not much preparation for the weekend on the river had been started, but the day was still young.

"He's in the shower," Ben replied. "Guess I kept him up too late last night. He just woke up a little while ago."

Erik shook his head and grinned. Sometimes he wondered how Troy managed to get himself to morning classes at college. Perhaps he had a dependable roommate, or perhaps his self-discipline improved during the school term.

"You and Troy can go to the *IGA* and get some groceries,"

Ben said, "...while I load the boat. I've got everything right here from last time." He dug his wallet from his back pocket and pulled out a twenty-dollar bill. "Here... take this. If we each chip in twenty bucks, we should have plenty for the weekend. Just don't let Troy buy out the whole store."

When they returned with the groceries, Ben was securing a canoe, upside down, on top of the johnboat.

"What's with the canoe?" Erik asked. "Where did that come from?"

"From behind the garage," Ben replied. "Thought it would be good to take along this time."

By the time they ate a good breakfast, packed their clothes, filled the coolers with plenty of food and drink, and got everything loaded into the boat, it was mid-afternoon. And by the time they reached their paradise camping island, it was nearly five o'clock.

The gear was taken ashore and the three worked like so many beavers fixing up their camp. Troy seemed a little more anxious for the supper to begin, and kept suggesting they should have done that first.

"You'd think we'd have to conduct a funeral out here because you died of starvation!" Ben joked. There was always jovial talk among the three at times like this, as they had now cemented in place a strong fraternity. Their fondness of each other allowed it. But if asked, even Ben and Erik would have had to admit that there was no part of an outing that suited them better than preparing a meal, or more accurately, disposing of it after it was cooked. There was just something special about food prepared over an open campfire. With appetites whetted to a keen edge by fresh air and freedom, they could hardly wait for the feast.

With huge burgers, a pot of pork and beans, and a jumbo bag of potato chips, it was more than pleasant to sit there, looking out upon the broad river and enjoying the feast. The cool and soothing breeze that came sweeping across from the distant shore seemed to be a different kind than any they ever felt at home – so much do surroundings have an effect on things. No one seemed to be in any hurry for this to end.

"Talk about your banquets," remarked Erik as he chomped on his burger. "This beats anything ever invented. I wouldn't trade places with a king, right now."

"My sentiments, exactly," echoed Troy, as well as he could with his mouth crammed full.

The sun finally dipped below the Iowa hilltops and the trees were partly lost in the gloom of coming night. The busy sounds of the river fell silent. All the high-powered speedboats had headed into ports. Even the blackbirds that had earlier been tuning up for their evening carols were quiet. The stillness of the natural environment was very soothing, but there was something disturbing about it, too. Not far away lay the enemy camp that protected secrets they needed to discover. But they were not quite certain what would happen next. There were, they calculated, at least several hardened men connected to this operation that were utterly unscrupulous, and probably wouldn't think twice about taking a human life. Any confrontation with this gang would certainly be dangerous, as they obviously possessed an arsenal of deadly weapons. The situation demanded subtlety and cunning rather than daring and brute force.

"When it gets really dark," Ben said, "I wanna take another look around on that island." He briefly scanned the faces of his companions to see if he had aroused any voluntary escorts. They were listening intently to his words, but they didn't realize he was looking for a verbal response, and they said nothing.

"You don't have to go with me if you don't want to," Ben finally added.

"Don't be crazy," Erik blurted. "I'm going with you."

"Of course, we're going," Troy added. "It's too dangerous for you to go alone."

"Well then," Ben said. He hesitated as he looked alternately at Troy and Erik. "We should get ready."

They all went to the tent and changed into dark colored clothing. Ben tucked his trusty .22 pistol in his belt, and when Erik stuck a revolver in his belt, Ben couldn't help but notice. "Hey! What's that?"

"A thirty-eight."

"Where did you get that?"

"Remember that night when they locked me in a room in the house in Genoa?"

"Yeah."

"Well, this is the gun I took from the guy in the hallway. I stashed it in the trunk of my car, and that's where it's been ever since."

Ben took the revolver in his hands to examine it under the light of the camp lantern. "Saturday night special," he said.

"Huh?"

"Serial number's been removed. It's probably stolen."

"Why doesn't that surprise me?" Troy joked.

Ben flipped the cylinder open to expose six live rounds of ammunition, closed it and handed the weapon back to Erik. "Be careful with that thing," he advised. "I'm kinda glad you have it now, but after this weekend, I'd get rid of it if I were you."

"Get rid of it? How?" Erik asked.

"Like... at the bottom of the river somewhere."

Erik stared at the shiny black revolver in his hand. He had held it only once before – the night he had escaped from captivity – so he had not grown fond of it. He thought it wouldn't be difficult to drop it into the river channel on the way home after the weekend.

They all took off their shoes, rolled up their jeans legs, and waded alongside the johnboat out into deeper water where they jumped aboard. Ben started the motor and ran it at just above a quiet idle all the way to the point at the end of the "enemy" island. By that time, their feet were dry enough to put on socks and shoes.

They pushed through the forested island, and even though the moonlight was an asset, they encountered a little navigational difficulty. First, an unnoticed log threatened to trip them, and then a hanging vine tried to choke them outright.

At one point, Ben called a halt as to ascertain any sounds that might indicate the presence of busy workers – voices, a cough, or a sneeze, or any sort of sound that would betray the presence of human beings. Nothing of the sort seemed to come. Ben signaled to start again in a low whisper, and it seemed as though he felt a new confidence. They continued on, stepping softly as kittens and moving with greatest care toward the canal.

Then through the stillness, they heard a noise that was no part of nature. Ben held up a warning hand and they all stood motionless, listening. Plainly it was the sound of boats coming up the canal. The boys dropped to all fours and crept forward to the point where they had hidden from view the first time they were there. As they neared the canal, the bright moonlight revealed several boats moored along the bank of the lagoon, and two more were just arriving.

They counted at least fifteen men that split into groups, some working in dim lantern light at a task by the boats, some near the long, low, camouflaged shack, and some appeared to take stations along the lagoon as sentries. Within about an hour, all except the guards disappeared into the small building that must have been quite crowded with so many behind its closed door. All was quiet, but after a time, raised voices could be heard, although Ben, Troy and Erik were too far away to make out what they were saying. At one point, Ben thought it sounded almost like a religious chant.

Then the sounds stopped abruptly and all the men filed out of the structure and went to the boats. In a few minutes, the only ones left were the guards watching the half-dozen runabouts slowly disappearing down the dark canal toward the river. After quite some time, the guards gathered together but they stayed near the lagoon, as if they didn't intend to leave anytime soon.

Ben gave a signal to retreat. There was nothing more they would discover in the darkness.

They came out of the cover, looking on the moonlit river. Ben leading the way turned up the grassy beach and soon reached the little point with stunted trees and considerable brush where they had tied up the boat. Using paddles they got well away from the island before Ben started the motor and headed back to their campsite.

Saturday August 25

Next morning, Ben sat alone on their sandy beach. He had risen early as usual, leaving the other two asleep in the tent. Watching the sunrise as the world emerged from shadows of night was his favorite time of day, especially out here on the river. Now that summer was waning and the nights were getting cooler, he welcomed the warmth of a sweatshirt and jeans pulled over his T-shirt and shorts. He listened to a distant freight train roaring along on the Wisconsin shoreline, and then as the day started to brighten, the squeaks and squawks of the river fowl began as they skimmed over the water's surface. A family of mallards swam toward the beach, but abruptly changed course when they detected human presence.

Troy stumbled out of the tent and started making a fire. In a little while, the aroma of fresh coffee seemed to wake up the entire island. Ben sauntered up from his seclusion on the beach and while he poured a cup of the hot brew, Erik just seemed to materialize next to him and Troy, holding out his cup. "Mornin' guys," he mumbled.

They sat around the fire savoring the coffee and enjoying the fresh, cool morning air. Within an hour or so, it would be August hot again, and Ben knew another spy mission on the mystery island lay ahead. This time it would be in the light of day. He thought he should go alone, as one body would be less conspicuous than three. "Later on," he started to say, "I'm gonna go back over there... alone... and see if there's any activity today."

"It'd be dangerous to go over there alone?" Erik said.

"No," Ben returned. "It'll be easier for just one to stay out of sight... safer, actually. And I'll take the canoe. It's quieter, and you'll still have the boat if you need it."

After they ate a hearty bacon and eggs breakfast, Ben stripped off all his clothes and slipped on a pair of jungle camouflage trousers and shirt. He had bought them at an Army Surplus Store just because he thought they were "cool" and would make good camping clothes, but now he realized they could be put to good use.

Erik looked on as Troy approached Ben just before he got in-

to the canoe to leave. He threw his arm across Ben's shoulders
and softly said, "Be careful, Ben. Come back safe."

Ben returned the gesture but he didn't say anything. He stepped
into the craft, grabbed an oar and paddled it out of the shallow
water.

Trekking through the woods on the island would be less hazardous during daylight hours. Yet, Ben's heart raced with anxious
anticipation, and perhaps a little fear of what might happen if he
were spotted by the hostile occupants of the camp on the other
side of the lagoon. The mid-day temperature was quickly rising,
and already he was drenched in sweat.

It occurred to him as he paddled near the end of the mystery
island that all the traffic to and from the camp happened at night.
His own experience told him that no one would be apt to witness
a boat entering or exiting through the curtain during darkness.
So there was little chance that any of the enemy boats would use
the canal during the day. If he were to paddle the canoe up the
canal, he could get a better view of the camp.

Shortly after 11 AM Ben probed the bow of the canoe into the
curtain of reeds that hid the canal entrance. He found the opening and with only slight difficulty paddled through. Cautiously he
continued up the canal to the first bend, and then the next, dipping his paddle and taking it out of the water as quietly as if it
were a spoon in a cup of coffee.

After some distance he began to hear voices, and through the
trees beyond a point of land, he detected some movement. Ben
knew he was close to the camp. He stopped paddling and listened to the sounds of the island. The water rippled against the
side of the canoe, and from somewhere deep in the forest came a
spine-tingling screech. Ben's imagination veered off course for a
few moments as he thought he had heard the cries of Indians of
long ago, their ghosts returning to mourn for their lost warriors.
"No. It was just a bird," he reassured himself. In the air was the
smell of hatred for any intruders, and he knew this was still a
dangerous place to be.

Staying in the darkest shadows along the bank, Ben maneuvered his craft nearer the point where he could stay concealed, but where he had a clear view of the camp. He pulled the pistol from his belt and laid it on the floor of the canoe in front of him where it would be instantly ready. Except for a small fire burning at the edge of the lagoon, it appeared as though everything there was quiet. He had been there only a few minutes when he saw one of the men come from the shack carrying a large, empty wooden box. Ben instantly recognized it as being one of the crates he had seen them load onto the pontoon boat, and later lug into the shack. As the man came to the open spot where the fire burned, Ben recognized him, too, as one of the rifle-toting men he had seen here a few weeks earlier when he, Troy, and Erik had first discovered the canal and this camp. Now, the rifle was in a sling on the man's back. Not far behind him was the second armed guard carrying another of the crates. His rifle, too, was slung on his back.

With heavy hammers they knocked the boxes apart and broke the thin boards into small pieces, feeding them sparingly into the fire. They seemed to be quite cautious with the fire, not allowing the flames to flare up into a roaring blaze. One of the men stood vigilantly by the fire while the other went to the shack and soon returned with another empty crate.

After a couple of hours watching the slow, monotonous disposal of the boxes, the men shoveled the remaining ashes and hot coals into the water, leaving hardly a trace of the previous fire, and soon they disappeared into the woods beyond the shack.

Long after the men had retreated to their hideout, Ben remained silent and still, waiting for any further activity. None came. He gathered up the pistol and quietly paddled the canoe back down the canal.

Troy and Erik were at the beach waiting to greet him as he paddled the boat across the shallows. When the bow hit the sandy shore, Ben stood up, stripped naked and jumped into the water. "God, it was like an oven in those woods," he yelled, and then fell prone onto the sandy bottom. Raising his head up out of the water, he called out, "It must be a hundred and fifty degrees in there!"

The water looked rather inviting. Troy and Erik were already in swim shorts, so they jumped in, too. "I'm glad to see you back here safely," Troy said, and he waded over to Ben to give him a welcome home hug. Erik came over next to him and slapped a hand on Ben's shoulder. "I didn't hear any gunfire, so I guess they didn't see you there," he said in a near joking tone.

Ben sat up. "Well, whatever they were hauling to that island, they don't intend to haul back out… at least, not in those crates."

Troy and Erik stared at Ben questioningly.

"I watched them for a couple of hours, at least," Ben went on. "They busted up those crates and burned them."

"In the middle of a hot day?" Erik quizzed. "Why do you s'pose they don't burn them at night and use the fire to keep warm?"

"Fires at night might draw some attention. A small fire like they had today during daylight isn't noticeable," Ben speculated. "That's why all those other men came, worked, and left under the cover of darkness, when it was less likely to be seen entering or leaving through that curtain at the end of the canal."

"Makes sense," Troy said. "Got any new ideas about what they're doing?"

"No. But they sure were careful with that fire."

"Speaking of fire," Troy said, "I have a good one going, too. You hungry? My hamburger light is on."

Sunday September 9

Ben woke with an uneasy feeling. Then he remembered it was September 9th – only two days until King and his band of deviants were to dispense some evil act. He had tried to alert Sheriff Lowery, but Lowery had responded with little or no enthusiasm. Ben understood the reason: he had claimed King to be the man in a magazine photograph, that, to anyone else might seem a little far-fetched; and now, when he claimed that King and his followers were planning some act of violence, Lowery considered Ben to be inflicted with unwarranted paranoia. He needed to find some hard evidence that the sheriff would believe, and would, perhaps, take immediate action.

Troy planned to spend the entire day with Grandpa Ernest – it was Grandparents' Day, and Grandpa Ernest always enjoyed this special day with his only grandson. Now that Troy was living in La Crosse again and back at school, he would have less time to spend with his grandfather. Ben couldn't possibly interfere with that, no matter what the circumstance.

But he thought he could count on Erik, even though he felt a little guilty for dragging Erik into what seemed a situation that grew more dangerous as the days passed. Erik had continued to prove himself as a loyal friend, and once again, Ben was grateful that they were on the same team. As his powerful arms repeatedly separated his rigid body from the floor of the deck in a series of rapid, early morning push-ups, he noticed another figure appear beside him, proceeding with similar actions. He stopped for a few moments to peer sideways at Erik, and then continued at an even pace with the newcomer. After number 100, they both stopped and sat up. Ben stared curiously at Erik.

"You look surprised," Erik panted. "Hope you don't mind that I joined you."

"No," Ben replied. "Just wasn't expecting it."

"Well, you always seem to be in such great shape. Guess I should follow your example."

Ben smiled. "Well, I wouldn't say that you're in *bad* shape. I recall one night in a dark parking lot… there were four or five of them, and only two of us. You seemed to handle yourself pretty well."

A hint of redness colored Erik's cheeks.

"And then," Ben continued, "…what about the night you took that gun away from a guy that was supposed to be guarding you? No, I wouldn't say you're in such bad shape."

Erik realized just then that he could have found no better friend than Benjamin Hudson. All summer, Ben had been showing him the way to self esteem and confidence, and he felt indebted to him for that. But he said nothing. He just smiled.

They sat on the deck enjoying the crisp morning air for a while, both recognizing their admiration for each other, but neither of them saying any more. Erik detected his friend's restlessness, and he was quite certain he knew the reason for it. "We're still gonna try to find out what King is up to, aren't we?"

Ben turned his head toward Erik, breaking a trance-like stare into space. "Yeah, I've been thinking about that. We have to figure out what they're doing out on that island."

"We're running out of time. Got any ideas?" Erik knew they had tried so many times before, never gaining any positive results.

"It's just you and me, now," Ben responded. "After Troy spends the day with Grandpa Ernest, he'll have to go back to La Crosse for classes tomorrow."

"What d'ya think we should do?"

"Let's pack some food in a cooler, grab a couple of sleeping bags, and head down to the river. We'll just sort of hang around Genoa. Maybe we'll see or hear something."

Late afternoon found Ben's truck, boat and trailer parked on a side street in the river town. He'd parked here many times in the past, but his uneasiness remained. It was, perhaps, just the nervous tension that made him pass around the boat to see that everything was secure.

Erik was a bit on edge, too. There was always the strong possibility that members of King's gang were in the town, and that they would recognize either him or Ben – their identity was by no means secret to the enemy. A confrontation now was a dreaded thought, but ironically, it was also somewhat necessary.

They strolled along the streets with no particular destination in mind. A few people were coming and going at Captain Hook's Tackle Shop, and the bars and restaurants were filling with out-of-town anglers winding down after a splendid weekend of sport fishing.

"Isn't that the bar where Chet hangs out?" Erik asked as he pointed down the street.

"Yeah," Ben replied. "And he's probably there now. I think I saw his pickup." He wondered if there would be any point in talking with Chet. If none of the Chicago gang showed itself, perhaps it might be worth pursuing later. It was difficult to determine if they were present now, as there were so many cars with Illinois plates in town. But there were no cars in the driveway at Barrington's house, and so far, there had been no signs of activity there.

It had been dark for quite a while when Ben finally decided to give up the watch on Barrington's house. "Let's go find Chet," he said to Erik.

"But I'm not old enough to go in the bar."

"No one will say anything if you don't try to buy alcohol."

Knowing they could come face-to-face with their adversary at any moment, Ben pulled the door open with due caution and they slowly stepped inside the Den.

Behind those big front windows was where Chet had earned his playboy reputation and his nom de plume, "Charlie." This was where his "Angels" congregated and often received their "mission assignments," such as a group of them mooning the crowd through the front windows. He referred to The Den as his "other home" or, sometimes, "the office." A regular patron, Chet knew almost everyone coming through the door, and was on the best of terms with the bartenders and the owner. He was often called upon to help out behind the bar for a little under-the-table compensation, and because he was such a familiar face, the clientele thought he was on the payroll.

The place was dimly lit, which made the big screen TV base-ball game stand out. However, the crowd noise level mixed with a blaring juke box would have made it difficult to hear the TV. The crack of billiard balls occasionally split through the rumbling from a mob that seemed to be having a good time. Ben led the way around the horseshoe bar until he spotted a familiar face. As he and Erik strolled to a spot near the end of the bar, Chet caught a glimpse of them. "Heeeeeeey, Erik," he called out. Then in a less jubilant tone, but still with a smile he said, "Hi Ben."

Erik beamed a goofy smile, and Ben nodded an implied greet-ing, but before he could say anything, Chet began again. "Sorry to hear about your father, man. Any word about what happened to him yet?"

Ben shook his head. "No. Not yet." He could feel a hundred eyes staring at him, so he paused until the surrounding gawkers had turned back to their drinks and rowdy friends. "Chet, I know you probably don't like my dad much 'cause he fired you, but could we talk?" He stared a moment at Chet's beer glass, but to Ben's amazement, Chet didn't seem intoxicated at all.

Chet gazed around the immediate area. "Sure. There's an empty table over there. Can I get you guys a drink?"

"Just a couple of *Cokes* would be fine," Ben said quickly. He leaned toward Chet and said quietly, "Erik's not old enough to drink here."

Ben was still amazed that Chet hadn't slurred his speech, or staggered, not even a little, as he brought their drinks from the bar to the empty table where he and Erik sat. He was sure of seeing Chet's pickup earlier, so he was certain Chet had been there quite a while – long enough to be fully inebriated by now.

"No, Ben," Chet started as he sat down. "I'm not pissed off at your dad. Well, I was at first, but I guess he had a good reason to fire me. And it's just as well... I didn't care much for Peter... prob'ly wouldn't have stayed there anyway 'cause of him."

"So, do you know anything about the arguments Dad and Peter were having?"

"Nope. I knew they weren't gettin' along, and Stan was always in a bad mood, and I figured that was why he told me one day that if I kept coming to work hung over, he was gonna fire me."

"But you kept coming here every night and getting hammered anyway."

"Didn't make any difference to me then. I was gonna quit one way or another... 'cause of Peter."

"What about those guys from Chicago?"

"Well, I know a lot of guys from Chicago. Some of 'em are good, and some, not so good." Chet nodded toward the far side of the bar. "There's Cheky. He's from Windy City."

Ben glanced across the room to the man in his mid-50s, wearing a western shirt and a cowboy hat. He appeared to be rather harmless, but that characteristic might easily be tossed off like an old glove. "Who's he?"

"Cheky can get you almost anything you want... real cheap... guns, mostly."

"He's a gunrunner?" Ben gasped.

"Guess you could call him that, yeah."

"Well, what about Lenny King and the other guys who work for Peter now?"

"They bought a bunch of guns from Cheky a while back, but they're okay... once you get to know 'em."

Ben's eyebrows raised. He looked at Erik, and then back to Chet. "Guns? What kind of guns?"

"Hunting rifles, I s'pose."

"And how well do you know them?"

"They come in here quite often, and of course, I knew them from Hudson Trucking, so we get along pretty good."

Ben's eyes narrowed to slits. "Have they ever told you what they do out on the river?"

Chet gave a little chuckle. "River? Seems like they're working all the time. When do they have any time to be on the river?"

Ben shook his head. Chet didn't know those guys as well as he thought he did. "Excuse me," Ben said as he got up from his chair. "I have to use the bathroom."

When he left the toilet, he realized he was near the back door that opened to a parking lot. He thought he would get a little fresh air and headed toward the exit. He didn't notice the two men following him out.

After Ben had walked away in search of the men's room, Chet asked Erik, "Why all the questions?"

"Ben's kinda worked up about his dad. Can you blame him? And we have good reason to believe that King and his gang have something to do with it."

Chet hastily changed the subject, and from then on, they talked about their work at Bert Greer's Used Car Lot. A half-hour passed, and Ben had not returned. Erik kept looking around the barroom, trying to catch a glimpse of him, but it seemed he had just vanished. "I wonder where Ben disappeared to," he told Chet.

Chet just shrugged his shoulders. "Well, I don't know, but I have to get going. See ya at the shop."

Erik sheepishly hustled to the men's room, thinking that Ben had perhaps fallen ill and was still in there. He found the room empty, and he, too, discovered the back door, quickly making his way out to the parking lot. He scanned the lot, and then walked briskly between the rows of cars in a hasty search. But he found no one. He circled around the building to the street, looking in every direction as quickly and as thoroughly as possible. There was no sign of Ben. "Maybe he went back to the truck," Erik thought out loud, and commenced trotting to the street where they left the truck and boat.

Everything seemed undisturbed, just the way they had left it. There was no evidence that Ben had been there. Erik stared into all the dark corners and alleyways. The darkness beyond reach of the streetlamps magnified his sense of being in danger. He thought about the guns that Chet had told about, and it occurred to him that they could be trained on him at that very moment. He needed to get away, and it was then he remembered the keys in his pocket. He had carried Ben's spare key on his key ring ever since the flat tire incident and Ben had never asked for it back. He fumbled with the key to unlock the door, rapidly jumped into the driver's seat, closed and locked the door. He thought of just waiting there for Ben to return. Surely, he would come to the truck. But then Erik thought about those guns again, and realized he was a sitting target. He would be safer on the move, looking for Ben, and definitely safer in the truck than on foot.

When Ben came to, he found himself lying on a wooden bench in a dreary, damp cellar. His head ached and his wrists were sore from the cord binding them behind his back. Struggling, he accomplished to sit up, and then his head felt like it would explode. He sat there waiting for the pounding in his head to subside. His last recollection was leaving the back door of the Den, the two men jumping him from behind and then nothing but blackness.

As the pain eased and his eyes began to focus, he saw the dark, shadowy figure of a man across the room, and behind him, at the foot of wooden steps, hung a single, bare light bulb that glowed an eerie radiance. The man was just a silhouette, but Ben recognized Lenny King.

"So it amounts to this, my adventurous young friend – you are at last in my power, absolutely, without the remotest chance of escape or of being rescued. Make no mistake about it, Mr. Hudson. You will no longer interfere with our operation. This time I will not delegate such business to other people."

Even though his hands were bound and he felt rather helpless, Ben refused to give this man the satisfaction of knowing he was afraid. And he was afraid – there was no denying it. But mingled with his fear was another emotion – disgust that he had allowed himself to fall victim to this fiend.

"You are a fool, Mr. Hudson, just like all Americans," King sneered. "You have no brains. It really gives me little satisfaction to defeat a man of your mental caliber – you fall so easily."

"Untie me, Lenny, and then we'll see who falls easily." Ben tried desperately not to let any anger show in his voice.

"I am perfectly willing to admit that up to now, your extraordinary vendetta against me and my interests has produced a certain amount of success. But I think you will agree that it has been due mostly to the element of luck, and perhaps with a little recklessness that is the result of your inability to measure the true value of risk."

It seemed to Ben that Lenny King suspected something that didn't exist – Ben's knowledge of King's agenda. He *didn't* know, but maybe King was about to let something slip out.

"You are a failure, my friend, and I hope you realize it. I know your kind well. You are one of those young, stupid, muscular, brainless creatures who think the most important matter in life is to be a sportsman and a good fellow. You live in luxury and wear fine clothes, but you give no thanks, nor do you pay the price."

This was all confusing to Ben. Lenny's words didn't make sense. But then, Lenny King was appearing more like a madman as the minutes ticked by.

Lenny went on. "And just because my beliefs are not your beliefs, and my convictions are not the same as yours, you not only judge me and my people, but you actually step in and attempt to stop my actions!" His voice that had begun quietly and calmly had grown shriller as he proceeded, until his last words were almost a scream.

"Just what are your beliefs and convictions, Lenny?" Ben spoke calmly. "They appear to be morally and legally questionable."

"My convictions are obedience to Allah, the great one. And who are you to be the arbitrator of my behavior? What qualification do you possess that entitles you to question my morality or decide the legality of my actions?"

"In case you're not aware, Lenny, holding another person prisoner is not exactly legal."

"What is the American saying? All is fair in love and war? Well, you young puppy, what do you mean by playing spy and following me about?"

"I am simply trying to find out what happened to my father," Ben said, remaining as calm as he possibly could under the stressful circumstance. "And I believe you had something to do with his disappearance."

"Your father was interfering, too, just as you are. But he is a coward, and he disappeared on his own accord. I know not where he is now."

All the while during their conversation, Ben had been working at the cord binding his wrists behind his back. He could feel a little slack. In this dim cellar light, Ben was quite certain that in the shadow cast by the table where he sat on the bench, King could not possibly notice his slight movements. One hand was nearly free, and once he managed to slip the rope off, he would remain in his present position and wait for the right opportunity.

If King was speaking the truth about Stan Hudson's disappearance, Ben thought, there might be reason for renewed hope that he was still alive. And distancing himself from association with this band of demons was not cowardly – it was, perhaps, the wiser choice, as Ben was beginning to realize. But at this moment, he hoped he could lure King closer. His wrists were free. He had never skirmished with King, but King was no bigger than any of the others, and he certainly didn't appear any tougher.

Ben felt confident that his fighting ability would be far superior to King's, providing there was no weapon to increase the odds. "I think *you're* the coward, Lenny," Ben taunted. "Think you're pretty tough, don't you, saying all that stuff to a man whose hands are tied. Yeah, Lenny, you're really a tough guy."

Lenny King had been perched on the edge of another table across the room, confident of his complete control. But now his captive was exhibiting some belligerence, and it irritated him. He stood and started stepping toward his prisoner.

For an instant, Ben enjoyed his success in drawing King nearer. He kept on taunting. "You know, Lenny, my friends will come looking for me. They know where I am."

Lenny stopped halfway across the floor. "I am not afraid of your friends. We are well prepared for any more intruders."

"You're still a coward, Lenny," Ben teased.

With that Lenny stepped to within a couple of feet from Ben as an unholy expression took command of his face. This was just what Ben had hoped. Lenny, unaware of his free hands would not anticipate the need for protection against retaliation from a bound man. His guard would be down, and Ben could detect no weapon. He positioned his feet, flexed his muscles in readiness for an effective strike at the last possible moment. As Lenny drew back a clenched fist with the look of intending to inflict a blow to quiet the vocal torment, Ben concentrated on his opponent's movement, and at the precise moment of the greatest vulnerability, when King had little or no chance to reach for a weapon, he sprung toward King with rattlesnake swiftness. They both went down with a thud, and Ben wasted no time in gaining control, pinning Lenny on his back on the damp floor. When he saw his chance, Ben delivered a stunning blow to Lenny's jaw with his right, and readied for another with his left. But he had disabled King enough with the first hit, as he lay limp and moaning. Ben heard hurried footsteps on the floor above, as if the noise of the scuffle had alerted others to come to Lenny's aid. Leaving his downed adversary in the middle of the floor, Ben ducked into the deep shadows behind the stairway.

Two men, Wolf and Hollister clamored down the steps

and rushed to King's side. While they still had their backs to the stairs, Ben darted up the steps and literally crashed through the doorway at the top. He quickly spotted the front entrance at the far end of the hall. As he sprinted across the lawn and down the steep driveway to the street, he thought that, perhaps, Lenny King had been partially right – Ben *was* lucky – that these guys were lousy wrestlers.

"We'll chase him down," Hollister said. "We'll get him."

Trying to shake off the dizziness, King grabbed Hollister's arm, stopping him. "Don't bother. He's only looking for his lost father. He knows nothing about our operation. Let him go. He's no threat to us."

With all certainty that he was being pursued, Ben bolted along the dark streets, anticipating that Erik would be waiting for him at his truck. He had no idea what time it was, but the streets were deserted, including the spot where his truck and boat should be parked. He dared not linger there. King's troops would certainly be patrolling the streets and roads. He had to get out of sight and the best place he could think of was into the adjacent wooded hills.

The morning was about to emerge – Ben's favorite time of day when everything always looked fresh and new. But he couldn't enjoy the dawn as he usually did. His head still throbbed, and he knew the rigorous activity couldn't be helping the condition. Feeling confident that he had reached safety in the woods, he looked for a spot to sit and rest. Leaning against a tree with his legs stretched out in front of him, he closed his eyes.

Monday September 10

The sun had already burned off the early morning fog when Erik opened his eyes. He remembered sitting alone, waiting and hoping that Ben would show himself. He figured he must have dozed off just about sunrise, because he remembered the sky beginning to brighten. Parked at the Power Plant Boat Landing had seemed like the most logical place to wait, at least until daylight. But Ben still hadn't showed up, so now the logical thing to do was to cruise the area again. But a dozen slow passes through all the streets in the small town didn't produce the sight of Ben. In daylight, and with more people around, he didn't feel quite so threatened, so he parked the truck on the same street where it had been the night before. From there he would start a search on foot, seeking all the places he could not see from the street. He suspected that Ben might have encountered another assault, and he could be lying helpless almost anywhere.

Erik had covered every alleyway, empty lot, and obscure corner in the whole town nearly three hours later. He turned his focus on Barrington's big house against the hill. There were no cars in the driveway, but that didn't mean the house was unoccupied. In broad daylight, Erik thought it would be too risky to prowl there. But he could watch it from the woods along the pathway that led to the church.

When Ben woke up again, he rubbed his eyes and took a few minutes to study the surroundings. The trek here was a bit of a blur; he knew he had passed out from absolute exhaustion or perhaps the splitting pain in his head. But the headache seemed much less severe now. Recollection of captivity and the conversation with Lenny King haunted his thoughts. *"We are well prepared for any more intruders,"* Lenny had said. Erik was no doubt looking for him and would certainly suspect the probability of Barrington's house. If Lenny's words were reliable, then Erik could also be in critical danger.

Ben looked at his watch. There was a lot of daylight left. He felt confident that Erik would not have just left; he had more backbone than that. If Lenny and his henchmen were still at large and still searching for their escaped captive, it would be risky to be seen on the streets. But it was a risk Ben thought was necessary. He started down the steep hillside toward the town.

After sneaking from behind one building to another, Ben became conscious of the fact that onlookers might consider *him* the suspicious one. Standing tall and proud, but keeping a cautious, watchful eye, he marched on. The truck and boat parked in al-most the same spot where he had last seen it the previous night was positive indication that Erik *was* nearby. His wandering eventually found him by the church where the path through the woods to the backside of Barrington's house began. Categorically less hazardous than approaching from the street, he started up the path at a swift pace, and when the Barrington house was barely in sight through the brush, he found Erik resting against a tree, apparently asleep. Ben gently shook his shoulder. Erik's startled expression changed to instant relief with the sight of Ben.

"What happened to you last night? I've been looking all over for you!"

"Yeah, well, I got whacked on the back of my head and kidnapped. I woke up in the cellar of that house." Ben pointed. "I'll tell you all about it back in the truck." He helped Erik to his feet and they hustled down the path.

Ben explained the entire event of his capture and escape as he drove his truck the six miles north to the *Kwik Trip* gas station in Stoddard. There he filled the truck and boat gas tanks. Sandwiches, potato chips and *Cokes* satisfied the grumbling stomachs.

"So, what's your plan?" Erik asked. They were headed south again and he could see Ben's tension.

"Lenny King..." Ben said thoughtfully, "... referred to me as *an American*, like he is not. And he called it *their operation*, which has to mean the activity out on that island."

Erik stared at his comrade. "Are we going back out there?"

"I think it's the only way we'll find something that the sheriff will listen to."

"We're running out of time."

"I know. But we have to try."

Dusk was just about to cast its shadow on the river valley. Many of the fishermen still out on the river would soon be heading for the various landings, and it wouldn't be long until the people with the larger, high-powered pleasure craft would be taking advantage of a genuinely delightful evening for a moonlight cruise on the water. It was almost surprising that Erik should recognize two men in a small runabout – two men that could have just as well passed as fishermen returning from the backwaters. They were headed upriver toward the landings, and it didn't seem like they had noticed Erik staring at them as they sped by.

"Those were two of King's guys," Erik said to Ben, loud enough to be heard over the hum of the Mercury outboard. "And they looked like they were in a hurry."

Ben cut back the throttle, looked over his shoulder, and without too much contemplation turned the johnboat back toward the landing. By then, the runabout was well ahead, and he could follow at a safe distance. He expected the boat to go to the Fish Hatchery landing, but instead, it continued on upriver to the power plant. The driver beached the craft on the sandbar behind the dock, and into the weeds beyond the open sand he threw out a rope with an anchor attached. Ben and Erik watched from out in the bay as the two men jumped to shore, briefly checked the anchor's effectiveness, and then headed briskly up the walkway to the parking lot. Ben pointed the johnboat toward the sandbar on the opposite side of the dock. His pickup was parked just beyond the willow brush.

"What you thinking?" Erik asked as Ben stopped the motor.

"My bet is that those guys are headed for the house in Genoa. Maybe we can find out their plans with a little eavesdropping."

"How do you figure we'll get close enough?"

Ben peered up into the sky. "It's getting dark enough. We can sneak in through the woods behind the house. And you know which window to go to."

It was true – Erik was familiar with that house because of his harrowing experiences there. He was just a little apprehensive about returning, but he knew the grave importance of the mission. Something was to happen the next day, and from what he and Ben had learned of these sinister characters so far, it wasn't apt to be pleasant for anyone.

Ben drove his truck to the side street and parked next to the church. "C'mon. We'll walk from here… through the woods."

Erik jumped out and caught up to Ben, already past the church. By then, darkness masked their movement and they could easily approach the rear of the old house. By the looks of the cars parked in front, there must have been quite a gathering inside, as there were no signs of any activity outside.

Erik recognized some of the cars: the Lincoln Town Car and the Jaguars had been there the night he narrowly escaped from the attic room. And the car in which the two men in the boat had left the power plant landing just a few minutes earlier was there, too.

"There… that's the window we need to get close to," Erik whispered to Ben. He was pointing to the window casting a dim, yellow light out onto the side yard. Through the curtains they could barely see several figures moving about in the room, and Ben seemed confident that it was possible to approach that window without being detected by anyone inside. He led the way through the shadows to the wall at the rear corner of the house, and then on hands and knees, they crept across the flowerbed that garnished the foundation. They stopped just below the lighted window. The smell of sweet smoke from a bubbling hookah drifted out the screened opening and muffled voices were heard among the clinking ice cubes in glasses. Ben rose up just enough to attempt a glimpse at the room's occupants. Eight or more men sat around a large oak table, and there were others standing around the room. Ben only recognized a few of them as some of Barrington's men, but the others were total strangers. Most of them wore black beards, and all were well dressed, some in business suits.

"Gentlemen," a suited man at the head of the table said, apparently attracting the attention of the whole group, as the room abruptly fell into silence. "I shall not detain you for long tonight. You all have your instructions, and I am perfectly confident in your ability to carry them out without any further advice from me. But this is our last opportunity for discussion before our operation begins, and it may be well to make certain that everything is understood and that we are properly prepared."

He paused to light a cigarette. For all the emotion in his level voice, he might have been addressing a committee meeting at a tennis club. But considering his audience, it was quite obvious that here was a set of men of a very different caliber. They all bore the unmistakable marks of those who see life in a different light, unscrupulous and devoid of kindness or consideration, full of hatred for society, ready to raise an offensive against mankind.

One of the men with his back to the window responded, "We are all attention, but these walls…" He waved his arm in an expansive gesture and quickly glanced around the room. "Are they…?"

"They are safe," replied the man at the head of the table with some shortness. "We have taken too many precautions for anyone in this little town to possibly be aware of our activities." Without lingering further on the subject, he turned to the men who arrived by boat. "Are the explosives all prepared and ready to be picked up?"

"Yes," was the reply. "Each load is armed with a detonator, and each one is capable of leveling a city block, more than adequate to eliminate the locks and dams, provided the boats carrying them make impact at the proper places."

The leader of the group continued, "Very well. There are six boats on their way from the north right now. They are to pick up their loads from the island at midnight. That will give them enough time to be in position at the other dams upriver. Four more will come from the south at three AM to be in position at Harper's Ferry."

After another short pause, he continued. "The *Delta Queen* will pass through these locks about nine AM, barring any major delays. If she is delayed, we can strike at Harper's Ferry."

Another pause.

"My good Islamic friends… tomorrow we shall rejoice in our victory. We have prepared well for jihad… Allah is smiling and is waiting with our rewards. The American people will look upon all that happens tomorrow as a national disaster. They will panic, and there will be chaos. And we will have been successful in our crusade against them. Let us go now, and do what we must do. We should not keep Allah waiting too long."

There was a shuffling of chairs and feet upon the floor. Ben turned to Erik and whispered, "Let's get out of here… now!"

They found their way in the darkness, once again, back to Ben's truck and sat there in silence for a few moments, catching their breath.

What a shock! They had had suspicions all along of some evil plot, but this seemed almost unbelievable.   Those fiends were prepared for suicide missions to destroy several Mississippi River dams and locks, not to mention the grand *Delta Queen,* and, perhaps a thousand or more passengers would die. And the aftermath would be devastating – the entire river valley would flood in one huge, uncontrollable wave of destruction. And then navigation would cease as the river reverted back to a shallow, unmanaged channel. It would take years – decades – to repair such damage. And the lives lost could never be restored. How could this possibly be happening?

"Bombs," Ben muttered.   "They've been hauling explosives out to that island and making bombs… right under our noses."

"Yeah, and just think about what they plan to do with 'em. God, Ben! We hafta warn… somebody!"

Ben sat behind the wheel, staring through the windshield. He watched the black Lincoln rapidly pass through a distant intersection and disappear, followed periodically by the other cars they had seen parked in front of the old house. He wondered if Peter Barrington was aware of how his house was being used by his employees – *if* they were really his employees. He wondered if Peter Barrington knew how his trucks were being used… and his pontoon boat… used to transport explosives to make bombs that, in a few hours, would cause massive destruction and kill hundreds, maybe thousands of people.

"Ben!" Erik said, his voice elevated in excitement. "We have to do something, *and right now!* We have to tell somebody about this! Those guys have to be stopped—"

"And just who do you think is going to listen? Who are you gonna tell?" Ben stared briefly into Erik's troubled eyes. "There isn't even a full-time cop in this town, and you know what kind of luck I've had with the County." He looked at his watch. "And besides…" Ben started the motor, put the transmission in gear and stomped on the gas pedal. "There isn't time to try to explain it to someone. This is something *we* have to do."

Erik knew that Ben had been contemplating a plan of his own

ever since they left the old house. He was headed back to the boat landing, and he wasn't wasting any time getting there. As he turned off the highway and crossed the railroad tracks, Erik asked, "What's your plan? What are we gonna do?"

"We're going out to that island and we're gonna detonate those bombs where they won't hurt anybody."

"Are you crazy? Just how do you think we're gonna do that? We'll get killed!"

"No, we won't. I've got a plan. You're just gonna have to trust me on this, Erik. I'll need your help. A lot of lives are at stake, so don't give up on me, okay?"

No answer.

"Okay?" Ben repeated louder.

"Okay." Erik realized that Ben was dead serious about accomplishing what seemed like an impossible feat. He had to convince himself that it was for the good of the people, and that placing himself in this utterly deadly situation was going to be worth the effort. There was no changing Ben's mind.

The truck came to a screeching halt in front of the boat trailer that they had left in the landing parking lot. Ben reached across the cab, opened the glove box, and pulled out the .22 pistol. It wasn't much against the weaponry of the terrorists, but it was all they had. Then he dug in his jeans pocket, pulled out a lighter, tested it, and put it back in the pocket. He looked at his watch again. "We don't have much time, Erik." He looked deeply into Erik's eyes. "I'm desperately sorry to have gotten you into this, Erik, but are you with me?"

Erik nodded. "I guess it's too late to be having regrets now. We're in this up to our necks. I doubt that we have much choice in the matter," he said softly but with confidence. "Yeah, I'm with you."

"Good. I'll explain my plan on the way."

They hustled to the johnboat down on the sandbar, but before they pushed the boat back into deeper water, Ben shook both gas tanks to make sure they were still full, as he had left them. The terrorists' runabout was already gone. It was a faster boat, but it wasn't that boat that concerned Ben – he was more concerned about the six boats coming from the north to pick up the bombs from the island. If they arrived early, his plan might fail.

Speaking as softly as possible, but loud enough for Erik to hear over the drone of the outboard motor, Ben explained his plan to get to the shack on the island. They would follow the outlet stream from the backside of the island, just as Ben had done before. It would be extremely dark, but Ben was confident that he could lead the way. When they reached the camp, Erik would somehow cause a diversion to draw the terrorists' attention away from the shack long enough for Ben to get to it, and douse it with the gasoline from the boat tank. A good hot fire would detonate the bombs, but not before the terrorists would be scrambling to put out the fire, giving Ben and Erik time and an opening to escape.

There wouldn't be an opportunity to rehearse. There wasn't time to analyze each detail. They had to get it right the first time...no second chances.

Ben idled the motor through the backwaters around the islands. He hated to go so slow, but he didn't want the sound of the motor to alert the enemy on the island. Noise was apt to carry in this night that was crisp and clear and as still as death, except for the murmur of the breeze among the treetops and the gentle lapping of the river on the rocks along the shoreline.

They tied up the johnboat at the canal outlet. Ben lifted the spare gas tank out of the boat and set it on the rocks next to the water. He handed the pistol to Erik. "Take this," he said. "It'll do you more good than me. I won't have my hands free."

Erik shivered with the thought that he would even need a gun, but he took it. He would circle around through the trees near the lagoon, and staying hidden as well as possible, make some racket to draw attention. That would give Ben a chance to work on the backside of the shack, and as soon as he knew the terrorists were more concerned about a fire than they were about him, he would make his retreat to the boat, and he wouldn't have much time to get away once the fire started.

They could hear the distant growl of several boat motors as they clasped each other's hands in an emotional greeting that was either "good luck" or "farewell," and they both realized that it could be either. Without another word, they started into the black forest, sharing the weight of the gas tank.

When they had gone some distance, Ben noticed the tiny bit of light again, and he knew they were as close as he had been before. He stopped and let the tank slowly down to the ground. The boat motor sounds were a little more distinct now, as if they were among the islands. There was little time left. He put a hand on Erik's shoulder. "Okay. Let's do it," he whispered.

Erik stood motionless. "I don't know if I can."

The motors were getting louder.

"Sure you can. I'll see you back at the boat." Ben picked up the tank again and stepped away from Erik. He stopped and turned to see if Erik had yet moved at all, but he only saw a black figure moving away toward the lagoon.

Ben knew it had only been a few minutes, but it seemed like hours. He had worked his way a little closer to the shack, but he could hear voices, and if he could hear them, they might hear him, too, so he stayed still, listening for his cue. The motors sounded as if they were at the far end the canal, and he couldn't tell for sure how many men were there at the shack waiting for the boats to arrive, but so far, he had only been able to detect two.

He thought he saw a flicker of light in the direction of the canal. The boats were approaching. "Come on, Erik," he whispered. Now a steady, solid red and green bow light appeared as the lead boat drew nearer, and then a loud CRACK, as if a small log had been thrust onto a tree trunk. Immediately, the two guards at the shack sprang to action, shining a powerful flashlight beam across the lagoon into the trees. He could hear, too, the click, click of automatic weapons being readied to fire. He prayed for Erik's safety, but he knew what he had to do. As the two men advanced toward the lagoon, Ben quickly and quietly trotted to the side of the shack away from them, removed the cap from the tank and started pouring the gasoline over the wall that was camouflaged with weeds and brush. Although he couldn't see them from where he was, he could hear the boats approaching –

it sounded like at least three – and now there were several voices raised. Erik was in danger, and he had to make his next moves quickly and effectively. With about a quarter of the gas remaining in the tank, Ben poured a line of the fuel on the ground as he retreated away from the building. When the tank was empty, he stopped. He estimated the distance to be about fifty feet. He briefly studied his position so he knew in which direction to run, dug the lighter from his pocket, and just as he was about to spin the striker wheel, his nervous hand dropped the lighter to the ground. Frantically, he stooped down, groping for the missing lighter. He heard gunfire – four or five rapid shots. Patting the ground all around him, his left hand found the lighter. He grabbed it firmly, and this time carefully spun the striker. The little yellow flame had only shone for an instant when Ben lowered it to the ground where the gasoline trail ended. The fuel ignited with a loud whoosh, and the blue flame raced toward the building. Ben watched it only as long as it took for the back wall of the shack to explode into flame, and he dashed off into the woods toward the edge of the island and the waiting boat.

The blaze was lighting his way now, making it easier to maneuver through the trees. As he ran, he thought about Erik – had he escaped? Or had the gunfire kept him pinned down, unable to get away? Or worse yet... he didn't want to think of it.

Ben wasn't far from the shoreline where the boat was tied, and here the flames of the fire weren't casting much light. He wondered how long he dared wait for Erik before he would start the motor and head for safety. Just as he was thinking that, he collided with another moving body, and in the next instant he felt himself tumbling into the dirt and weeds. Before he was completely at rest, he scrambled to his feet again.

"Ben?"

"Erik?"

They didn't take time for pleasantries, but fumbled with the mooring rope, pushed the johnboat into the water, and jumped aboard. Ben was at the controls and had the motor running by the time Erik could get to the other seat. They stared toward the heavily forested shoreline for just a moment, seeing the glow of the fire getting brighter.   In the excitement, it seemed like they had passed through a lifetime in a few minutes, the events tumbling over one another, helter-skelter.   Ben jabbed at the throttle lever and brought the craft into plane just as they were clearing the end of the island.   As he pointed the boat toward the far side of the next island, Erik watched the glow behind them become more brilliant, and he could only imagine those men scrambling to save the building – or scrambling to save themselves.   But he didn't care which they were doing.   He was subconsciously aware of his own tenseness, as if he were bracing himself for a shock.

And then everything lit up around them in a rapid series of strobe-like flashes, and a heartbeat later came the corresponding series of shattering booms and vibrations that shook the earth. Ben slowed the motor down to an idle and the boat settled into the water just a little short of the point of their camping island. He and Erik stared back over the trees to see the giant yellowish fireball disperse into the sky as the rumble echoed between the bluffs on either side of the river, and then, for a few moments, everything was quiet.

But as with any hastily laid plan, one effect from the blast was not expected, nor had it even been thought of.   Ben had figured the island to be far enough away from just about everything and even a large explosion would be rather harmless and do little or no damage outside the perimeter of the island.   But he had not considered the effect it would have on the water.   A tidal wave on the Mississippi River was unheard of – until now.   They could hear the roar, but there was no glow from any fire – the explosion had scattered and extinguished what little remains of the burning wooden structure was left.   And then the roar identified itself more like the sound of ocean surf, lapping violently along the shoreline of the island as it heaved a four-foot high wall of river water crashing through the darkness toward the little boat. By the time Ben realized what was happening, there was no time to get the boat moving fast enough to race ahead of the wave. He revved the motor, but even before the boat had started to react, the wave tossed it as if it were a toy, carrying it the entire distance to the shoreline and driving it into the weeds and mud.

Almost immediately, what seemed like the entire Atlantic Ocean splashed over it as a second wave hit just as Ben and Erik leaped and stumbled to the bank, trying to escape the rage.

In only the time it would take to count ten, the roaring stopped. The adjacent islands had absorbed the furious waves, and now there was nothing more than the stillness of a river night surrounding the two as they stood peering into the eerie darkness. The events of the past hour tumbled around in Ben's head like towels in a dryer, and he could only wonder at the fate of the men they'd left behind on the island. He could hear no boat motors – only the ringing in his ears from the deafening blast. His whole body felt numb, as if he were in a dream and couldn't wake up. And then his physical senses slowly came alive, and he realized his wet clothes and his chilled body. Erik was a motionless statue beside him.

Survival would become only a moderate concern; the night would be cold, but not so cold as to be deadly. Their only transportation – the boat – lay in the weeds, swamped, and as he waded through the tall grass and muck to reach it, Ben thought it would be doubly miserable to attempt getting it worthy of travel again, in the dark. He reached over the side, felt under the seat, and discovered two soaked sleeping bags. He grabbed the waterproof canvas tarp that was always there for use in emergencies. This certainly qualified.

"Let's go find our campsite on the other side of the island," he told Erik. "We'll build a fire and get warmed up a bit."

Tuesday September 11

Dawn's first bit of light found Ben waking to the sounds of outboard motors buzzing around their island camp like a confused swarm of bumblebees, but he knew none could be very close because of the shallow water. He blinked a few times and tried to shake away the grogginess. Erik seemed to still be asleep, but he, too, was now beginning to stir as the roar of a small airplane passed overhead at a very low altitude. Ben stared up toward the sky, but the thick canopy of tree branches blocked out any visual sign of aircraft, and likewise, they were well concealed on the ground, too.

His thoughts abruptly captured the phenomenal events of the early morning hours – the fire; the tremendous explosion and the blinding flash; the wave of water that swamped his boat; the search for dry wood to build a fire for a little warmth; taking cover under the tarp that did little more than keep off the dew. It almost seemed odd to him that they had been able to fall asleep after their experiences of a few hours earlier. And now, he suspected that everyone who owned a motorboat – or plane – would be out trying to satisfy his curiosity of what had taken place. They would find nothing, he thought, except an expanse of water where that part of the island had been, as certainly, by now, the canal would have fed the void with plenty of river water, forming a lake upon the island. There wasn't much chance that anything – living or otherwise – could have survived a blast of that magnitude at ground zero, or perhaps, anywhere on that island.

The airplane made another pass, this time not directly overhead, but it sounded as if it were circling to make further survey of the area. Ben wondered if it could be a search plane, looking for him and Erik. No. No one else knew they were on the river, or would have any reason to question their whereabouts, unless they were discovered missing from home, and that wasn't too likely this early in the morning. But what if someone were to spot his swamped johnboat? That would certainly raise some eyebrows – that is, if the finders were, perhaps, searching for whoever was responsible for the blast. Or... maybe they were searching for survivors, or... or bodies.

Ben sat up, and then reached toward Erik, still curled up, clutching the tarp wrapped around him, trying to gain even the slightest amount of warmth from it. He gave Erik's shoulder a gentle little nudge. "Erik. You awake?"

"Yeah, but I'm freezing. Can we build a fire?"

Ben had always been able to withstand the cold a little more than most people. But even he felt chilled and miserable, and he could understand Erik's discomfort on this chilly September morning. He threw back the portion of tarp covering him, found a few sticks and leaves for kindling, touched a flame to it with his lighter, and departed to gather some larger wood for a better fire. Within a few minutes, they were both huddled close to a crackling campfire, the tarp draped over their backs to retain the heat. Even Ben admitted the warmth of the fire felt pretty good. They sat there for a little while, still stunned by the night's developments. Their clothes were still damp, and it was no wonder why they were cold and miserable.

"Sounds like a lot of boats out on the river," Erik said.

"When I went looking for firewood I saw a bunch of 'em headed toward Mystery Island," Ben replied. "But I don't know that they'll find anything other than a hole full of river water."

"Yeah," Erik said. "I'd bet that island is kinda jizzicked."

Ben chuckled. He remembered the Maine expression meaning *ruined beyond repair*. "Destroyed would probably be more accurate," he said.

Erik nodded in agreement. "What d'ya think we should do?"

"Well, for starters, we'll have to get the water bailed out of the boat and try to sneak back to the landing."

"Why should we have to sneak?"

"Do you wanna explain to all those people out there what happened?"

"No… but what makes you think anybody will ask us?"

Ben thought about that for a few moments. Erik had a good point. They could blend in with all the rest of the gawkers, and no one would have any reason to suspect them of knowing any more about the incident than they did. The biggest challenge would be to get off this island without too many people noticing them, as they would have to spend some time bailing the water out of the boat, and that could attract some attention. But it was a risk that seemed miniscule compared to those already taken.

Ben glanced at his watch. It was just about 6:30. There was plenty of light now to assess the situation at the boat. It was a bit of a hike from the campsite to where the boat lay swamped in the shallow water on the other side of the island, so he suggested they get started right away.

They were well on their way when Erik stopped abruptly and

put a hand up to Ben's chest as a signal for him to stop too. "What's the date today?" he asked.

Ben thought for just a couple of seconds. "September eleventh," he said.

"Ya know?" Erik said with just a twinge of a smile. "It's my birthday today. Today, I am nineteen years old."

"Well, happy birthday," Ben responded. "We sure made some good fireworks to start off the day for you."

They started walking again. "Ya know," Erik said, "Ten years ago I thought I would be flying around in space by the year 2001, and here I am trampin' through a jungle on a Mississippi River island. And on my birthday, yet."

"And if you had it to do all over again? Where do you think you'd rather be?"

Erik didn't have to give it much thought. "Right here... with you... on this island."

Ben tossed a big grin at his friend.

With little difficulty, they managed to get the water bailed out of the johnboat. It wasn't deep enough to be over the top of the battery causing it to short out, and the motor had dried out enough so that with a little coaxing, it started and ran. Ben didn't see any obvious damage done by the miniature tidal wave other than a little mud left on the floor.

In the seven or eight miles back to the Genoa landing, they met at least twenty more small boats heading downriver, and while they waited at the landing for several more to launch, a couple of fellows, appearing not to be equipped for fishing, approached Erik at the end of the dock. "What's all the excitement about?" they asked. "What did you see out there?"

Erik just shrugged his shoulders and shook his head, glancing toward the parking lot and hoping that it would soon be Ben's turn to back his trailer down the ramp. They had decided beforehand not to start any conversations with anyone there – one would lead to another, and they didn't want to be there any longer than was absolutely necessary.

With the boat loaded and several sighs of relief, they were away from the landing. As they drove through Genoa toward the highway to home, Ben decided to stop. He was hungry and thirsty. They could have gone into the Big River Inn for a full-fledged breakfast, but Captain Hook's Tackle Shop would be open, too, and grabbing a cup of coffee and some donuts there would be just fine.

There seemed to be a lot of people out and about for such an early hour, and comments brought out in the open about the disturbance during the night were not in short supply. As Ben had surmised, the inhabitants of Genoa, and probably many other towns up and down the river, awakened at midnight by an appalling explosion that rattled most of the windows in the town, thought of the unbelievable notion of an earthquake. But those who happened to be awake when it occurred, though, agreed that a terrific flash of light had preceded it, and they had been inclined to believe it was a gigantic thunderbolt. For an hour or more the streets had been dotted with people discussing the phenomenon, but as it was not repeated, they had gone back to bed. It was at breakfast that the excitement rose high again in the early morning restaurants and coffee shops. Strange rumors were flying about. Some were embellishing the incident, claiming they had heard the hum of aircraft, and they were talking darkly about another war. Of course, most coherent people dismissed that idea – why would an enemy of the United States choose to attack such an unlikely location where there was nothing of strategic or economic importance to destroy? Few people could conceive an inkling of an idea that this was in any way related to the Gulf War of so many years ago but still fresh in their minds, although the concept did breed another tongue-lashing of the Government for its weakness in not dealing more firmly with the American foes.

Trying to reach the coffee and donut bar, Erik and Ben listened quietly to the comments and rumors while they shuffled through the biggest crowd they had ever seen inside Captain Hook's. They wanted to speak out, and tell these people that what they had heard and seen in the middle of the night was, indeed, the powerful force that had almost been successfully launched against them by a foreign terrorist group. They wanted to tell these people that they had diverted the disaster from occurring – a disaster that would have had the potential of destroying property and taking lives. But they remained silent. They were afraid to become involved right then. A better time and place, with a more appropriate audience would avail itself. But not now.

But at length, the rumor thickened in one particular direction, as soon as some of the spectators started returning from the explosion site, and it soon became generally known that a mysterious attempt had been made to blow up an island halfway between there and Lansing, with little evidence as to why, or who might have been responsible. Charter boats carrying curious adventure seekers were already arriving from up and downriver, and the Engineers at the locks had not seen so much activity all season.

"Good mornin' Boys," the man at the cash register said, eying the two coffees and donuts. "Out for a little fishing today?"

"Mornin,' Byron," Ben returned. "We're actually on our way back home." And before Byron could continue the conversation after he had counted Ben's change, Ben and Erik slipped out the door and headed to the truck parked across the street.

Forty minutes later, Ben stopped the truck in the driveway of his country home. Both he and Erik were glad to be there, and somehow, the comfort of a soft chair in dry, clean clothes seemed of the greatest importance. They each had a hot shower, donned fresh clothing, and converged in the living room.

They sat in silence a few minutes, and then Erik said, "Who should we talk to about this?"

"I guess I should probably call the County Sheriff, but I would imagine that he and every one of his deputies are down at the river..."

Just then, they heard the sounds of a car out in the driveway. Ben craned his neck to see Troy's black Buick stop in front of the house. The car had barely come to rest when Troy jumped out, headed for the front door at a dead run. This time he didn't bother to knock.

"Boy, am I glad to see you guys!" he said, nearly out of breath and almost in tears. I tried calling early this morning, and when I didn't get an answer, I got pretty worried."

"Why? What's the big deal?" Ben said, as if he didn't already suspect that Troy had somehow heard about the river incident.

"Turn on the TV... quick... you ain't gonna believe what's goin' on!"

Ben clicked on the television, and they all stared at the dark screen, waiting for a picture to appear. "What's happening?" Erik asked, his anxiety approaching a peak.

The TV picture brightened, revealing a big city skyline. The voice they heard, high-pitched from excitement, was an on-location news reporter recapping what had just taken place in New York City, and the scene was truly unbelievable: "Just minutes ago, our cameraman caught this terrifying sight – just a few blocks away, at the World Trade Center Twin Towers, here in New York, a jet airliner has crashed into one of the Trade Center towers..." And then a replay of the horrible event showed the plane flying directly into the huge, glass-covered building, resulting in a fiery cloud of smoke and flame bursting from the tower, emerging like the mushroom cloud of an atomic bomb blast. The live sound picked up by the reporter's microphone revealed the terrified screams of people on the street as the camera briefly scanned the immediate area, people running in chaotic disorder. Some faces showed terror, and some showed disbelief of what their eyes were seeing, and it wasn't difficult to see the general feeling of those people turning to sheer panic.

The camera was once again focused high on the tower with smoke billowing from the upper third. And as if the shock of that sight had not registered, a second plane came into view for only a second before it, too, was swallowed up by an explosive ball of flame and billowing smoke as it made its impact on the other skyscraper adjacent to the one already struck.

The news commentators immediately speculated that this was a planned terrorist attack, and then the emotional drama intensified beyond all imagination when they reported that almost simultaneously a third jet had crashed into the Pentagon in Washington, D.C., and a fourth came down in a remote area of Pennsylvania, apparently failing to reach its intended target.

The three boys stood in front of the TV, staring, hardly breathing, and hardly believing the events unfolding before their eyes. Then Troy finally spoke. "When I heard about the explosion down on the river this morning, I thought I should call you right away, and— "

"How did you hear about that?" Ben asked.

"It was on the TV news early this morning, long before all this started. I happened to catch it in the Student Union while I was having breakfast. When I didn't get an answer here on the phone, I came right home. You weren't here the first time I came over, and I was just about goin' nuts." Troy pointed to the TV. "There! Listen!"

The broadcast had switched back to the local station live from the Channel 19 studios high atop the bluff overlooking La Crosse. "… It is not known at this time if the tremendous explosion that occurred at approximately midnight on an island in the Mississippi River just below Lock and Dam Number Eight at Genoa is related in any way to the attacks in New York and Washington… and in case you have just tuned in…"

"They don't know," Ben said.

"They don't know what?" Troy asked.

"Don't you see? This was all supposed to happen at the same time. If we hadn't stopped them, right now there would be no lock and dam at Genoa, or La Crosse, or Trempealeau, and probably the one at Harper's Ferry, too. The whole valley would be flooded, and all those poor people on the *Delta Queen* would have been blown to bits."

They watched the local broadcast showing video footage, taken from an airplane, apparently in the early morning light. It was pictures of the island where the explosion had occurred – their "Mystery Island" – revealing the huge gap between two smaller islands that until a few hours ago had been one large landmass.

"That was the plane flying over us this morning," Erik said.

"You mean," Troy interrupted, "You were there when they were taking these videos?" He wasn't entirely aware, yet, of his buddies' involvement – that they had actually detonated the explosives on the island.

They didn't hear the car pull into the driveway and park behind the boat. Nor did they notice the County Deputy briefly inspecting the interior of the craft. Then a knock on the front door drew their attention. Ben went to the door and opened it. Somehow, when he saw Deputy Roger Owens standing on the porch, he knew why he was there, but he hadn't determined how the police had connected him to the blast on the river.

"Mornin' Ben," the deputy said.

"Mornin' Roger."

"Ben, I really hate to bother you right now... I know this is a pretty tense time for everyone." He noticed the TV was tuned in on the current events.

Ben nodded and glanced toward Troy and Erik and the TV. "Yes, I guess it is," he agreed.

"The reason I'm here," Deputy Owens began, "Is... well, I guess you know about the explosion down on the river last night... I see you have the TV on."

"Yeah, I know about it."

"Well, the officers investigating the scene have found the wreckage of several boats in the immediate area, and they've recovered several bodies. They also found a gas tank – it was kinda beat up, but they found your name scratched in the paint."

Ben had forgotten about that one little detail.

"We were afraid you might've been one of the casualties," the deputy went on. "But now that I know you aren't, can you explain how it got there."

"Yes, Roger," Ben said, letting out a sigh of relief. "I can explain that to you. Come on in."

Friday September 14

Even after several days, the initial shock of the attacks on Washington and New York had not completely faded from the American public's eye. TVs and radios were constantly tuned in on the current events. Tensions escalated as the American people learned the details of how such a monstrous, barbaric act could have possibly happened on homeland soil. Speculations ran rampant while citizens sat at the edge of their seats with fearful eyes focused to imminent war with an enemy they did not know.

Although the national news of the more successful attacks on the eastern seaboard overshadowed the Midwest failure, the people of southwestern Wisconsin – especially those who lived near the Mississippi River – were aware that their safety had been jeopardized. They were relying on their own local resources for the accounts of what had really happened, right in their own back yard. The county sheriff was withholding much of the information from the news media while further investigation continued, but the people knew the staggering truth that the island explosion was a misdirected force that had been intended to destroy lives and property. And they were grateful to the unidentified individuals who had prevented it from occurring.

Not much business was conducted at Bert Greer's used car lot, but Erik did his best to keep busy, trying to avoid thinking about how near he had been to death. He and Ben had received strict orders from the sheriff not to discuss the incident with anyone until the investigation had progressed to some conclusive results. There was no telling how long that would take, and he feared he could not withstand the anxiety. He didn't know whether to feel frightened or relieved when he saw the sheriff's squad car parked in the driveway as he arrived home after a short day at work.

Ben met him at the door, and by the grin on Ben's face, Erik suspected there might be some good news. "Erik," Ben greeted him. "Glad you're home. There's someone I want you to meet."

Following Ben, Erik stepped cautiously into the living room and eyed several men sitting and standing. Among them were Sheriff Kent Lowery, Deputy Roger Owens, Troy, and another man Erik didn't recognize. Their conversation had stopped as they watched him enter. Ben led him straight to one of the men who rose from the couch, turned and stood beside him with his hand on the man's shoulder. "Erik," Ben said with a beaming smile. "This is my dad, Stan Hudson."

Erik stared, somewhat in awe, at the stranger before him. Stan Hudson, dressed in casual slacks and a crisp white shirt, was a tall, slender, handsome man. When he smiled and extended his hand, Erik saw and older replica of Ben.

"Well, young man," Stan said in a pleasant tone. "So we meet again."

Erik shook his hand with growing bewilderment. "Again? I don't think I've had the pleasure…"

"Don't you remember speaking to me in Genoa? You won the race that night."

Erik's face lit up. "Yeah, now I remember! I caught up to you by the church. I thought you were just a bum. I didn't recognize you now without your beard and that floppy hat."

"Yes, I suppose that's true," Stan replied. "It's too bad that my disguise didn't help me be as good a detective as you fellows."

"You mean… you've been in Genoa all this time?"

Stan nodded. "Sharon at the Genoa House put me up in the apartment over the gift shop. She was kind enough to keep my identity secret, and she even brought groceries in for me."

"But, why…"

Sheriff Lowery stepped in. "Stan was in danger. Barrington thought he knew too much, and there was a good possibility that he might've been murdered. So he had to fake abduction and stay out of sight."

"It was all pre-arranged," Stan added. "Otis picked me up at the old shop where I left my pickup… so somebody would find it without me."

"Why did you let me believe all this time that he was missing?" Ben asked the sheriff. "Why didn't you let me in on this?"

The sheriff took a deep breath. "We couldn't take the chance that Barrington would find out Stan was still around. If he thought you really believed Stan was missing, then he'd let his guard down a little."

"So, are you going to arrest him?" Erik asked.

"He's already behind bars on numerous charges – forgery, embezzlement, and conspiracy, just to name a few. And when we get done with him, Cook County in Illinois wants a piece of him, too."

"So," Troy interjected. "...Barrington was behind this all along?"

Sheriff Lowery rubbed his chin. "To be perfectly honest, we knew nothing about the terrorist activity. It remains to be seen if Barrington had anything to do with it at all. And Ben? I guess I should've paid closer attention to you. Leonard King – and that's not his real name – was one of the bodies recovered near the blast site. At least three others were Barrington's employees."

"So, what happens now?" Ben asked. "The terrorists killed in the blast weren't working alone..."

Sheriff Lowery interrupted. "The FBI and CIA are handling it from here. From the information you gave us that day, they are already rounding up more of this gang in Chicago. Of course, they'll want to talk to you some more, I'm sure."

"How 'bout that?" Troy mused. "You're a genuine hero."

Ben leaned toward Erik and put a hand on his shoulder. "Don't forget Erik. I couldn't've done it without his help."

Ben turned to his dad. "Guess I won't be going back to Colorado this fall."

"I meant to talk to you about that," Stanley replied. "Now that Peter is gone and I have control of the company again, I think I could use a little help. What'ya say we change that sign above the door to Hudson & Sons?"